Sherlock Holmes: The Adventure of the Cold-served Revenge

by Petr Macek

Paperback ISBN 9781780926599
ePub ISBN 9781780926605
PDF ISBN 9781780926612

Published in the UK by MX Publishing
335 Princess Park Manor, Royal Drive,
London, N11 3GX

www.mxpublishing.com
Cover design by www.staunch.com

CONTENTS

Foreword

Epilogue
Afterword

Foreword

The publishing sensation that I caused with my manuscript describing the case of Golem's shadow took a long time to die down. Indeed it was here that I detected the true reason for Holmes's retirement at the end of 1903, and thus finally eased my conscience. For many years I had been compelled to lie or at least mask the truth.

My promise to my publisher Mr Doyle, who had refused to print my work, still applied. I therefore undertook to write about another, less controversial case, but one that would still sate the public's hunger for the adventures of Sherlock Holmes, while at the same time offering something new and unexpected. I had no desire to return to the years that I had already minutely described in several previous books.

The events of the spring of 1911 still loomed. I was no longer contributing to *The Strand* and Holmes had retired from public life. At no time earlier had there been a reason to make the case public. Indeed, for a number of years, up to the end of the Great War, parts of the case had been kept classified. I trust, therefore, that the reader will forgive me that in the interests of several highly placed people related to the royal family I have changed several names.

I am aware of the shame of letting these days fall into oblivion. Although while living through them old memories returned to us, some of them were unkind. But there is one man above all who deserves to be remembered: he who put us on the chessboard of this case and almost gave us mate.

Dr John H. Watson, February 13, 1927

I
The Ivory Cigarette Case

Back when the new century was growing into its adolescent years, when motorcars were replacing hansom cabs and gas was giving way to electricity, Sherlock Holmes and I saw much less of each other. He was occupied with beekeeping at his country farmstead in Fulworth near Eastbourne in Sussex, and I divided my time between my medical practice and my wife[1]. The days when the famed detective and I would plunge into London's dank alleyways or struggle through the inhospitable marshes of innumerable counties in pursuit of a felon seemed irretrievably lost. Our intercourse was reduced to intermittent visits and only marginally more frequent correspondence.

At that time both of us were well into our sixth decade and enjoyed the dignity that was our due. On occasion, during my ambles through the city, I would stray inadvertently into Baker Street and pause nostalgically at 221B, where seventeen steps led to our old lodgings. But the number of steps was the only thing that had not changed. The apartment was occupied by new tenants; young people better adapted to their rapidly changing surroundings. Old buildings were being demolished and new ones were rising up in their place. Everything was being modernised. The explosion of building at the beginning of the twentieth century affected every aspect of life and trampled all that was old into the dust.

---

[1] This is the second or third Mrs Watson. The wedding took place on October 4, 1902. The first (or second) Mrs Watson, née Mary Morstan, died sometime between 1891 and 1894, perhaps on December 27, 1892.

But I am not one to bemoan time's ever-increasing pace or to linger in the past, with the exception, of course, of my literary accounts of our adventures. And so, on one of those visits to these parts, I only reminisced briefly about bygone glories before again returning home.

Indeed it was here that, quite unexpectedly, one of my last adventures with the great detective got underway. It began in the same way as many others; with a hastily written telegram sent in distress.

But this time there was one alarming difference: the telegram had been sent by our former housekeeper, Mrs Hudson, and directly concerned Sherlock Holmes!

My blood turned cold.

Alas those few words written on a slip of paper did not describe exactly what had occurred. Mrs Hudson only mentioned Holmes's dire health and urged me to come as quickly as possible. I gathered that he had probably suffered a coronary thrombosis.

I replied at once to expect me tomorrow and reserved a seat on the morning train to Sussex.

That night I could not sleep. To my knowledge, except for a touch of rheumatism that he complained of in his letters, Holmes did not suffer from any grave ailment. I must concede, however, that his lifestyle during our years together was a recipe for a coronary. The strain and stress and his generally unbalanced regimen must surely have taken their toll. But why had they culminated now? After all, in recent years his sole occupations had been tranquil philosophising, literary studies, and a bit of farming.

On the journey the next day, despite the breath-taking view of sun-bathed fields and pastures from my compartment, I was beset by troubled thoughts. I did not even read the morning *Times*, the front page of which was devoted to the latest crisis in Morocco. France and Germany were vying for it with unceasing persistence. Each was attempting to forge an alliance with England, which only heightened already elevated tensions in Europe. The recent military defeats had been a shock to England's self-confidence and had revealed the Empire's unpreparedness for war. The paper speculated that King Edward's[2] entente[3] had been an error that had led us away from our time-honoured Splendid Isolation[4]. The rest of the paper was full of tumultuous domestic reports: the Irish problem, suffragettes[5] and the demands of the working classes. Nothing new under the sun. Nothing to unburden my mind of its cares.

There was only one item all the way in the back of the foreign affairs column that piqued my interest, story about the violent death of the famous Italian factory owner Vito Minutti. He had been shot in his office right in the middle of the day and they only found his body several hours later. The culprit was being hunted by the police commissioner heading the

---

[2] Edward VII (1841–1910). He was the son of Queen Victoria and ruled from 1901 until his death. His successor was George V, who ruled during the time when the events in this book take place.

[3] An alliance between France, Russia and Great Britain, entered into in 1907 in response to the expansionist tendencies of Germany and Austria-Hungary.

[4] Great Britain's foreign policy at the end of the 19th century under conservative prime minister Benjamin Disraeli and the Marquess of Salisbury. The term referred to Britain's involvement in European affairs.

[5] A militant feminist movement that fought for women's rights. It was established in about 1900 and used extremist methods to achieve its ends.

investigation, who did not want to discuss suspects or motives. Clearly they were dumbfounded. Indeed, I had been infected by Holmesian scepticism towards the police and their work.

I only raised my eyes from Minutti's obituary as the train pulled into the station. A coach was waiting for me and immediately took me to Cuckmere Haven[6]. For those last few miles before reaching my destination I sat on the coach box next to the coachman as though on tenterhooks. My heart was racing. I feared whether I might be too late.

Good Mrs Hudson, who had taken care of Holmes for many decades and had even left her native London to follow him to the countryside, was already waiting at the doorstep. As soon as she spied us she waved her hand and hurried over to the coach.

"Doctor! Dear doctor, thank God, I am so happy that you are here," she cried, extending her arm towards me before the coach had even stopped.

"How is he?" I asked, in lieu of a greeting.

"The pastor is with him," she said, breathing heavily. At her age she tired quickly and any excitement exhausted her.

I hopped down from the coach and gently embraced the diminutive woman.

"Last rights?" I gulped.

"Not yet," she said, crossing herself. "Do not paint the devil on the wall or he will appear. Pastor Barlow is a friend of Mr Holmes; he runs this parish and often visits us. Today he

---

[6] According to Holmes researcher Christopher Morley, *Cuckmere Haven* is not the name of Holmes's farmstead, but the real name of the village of Fulworth, which lies between Seaforth and Eastbourne on the south slopes of the Sussex lowlands.

came in order to cheer him up a little. In truth yesterday evening I feared that Mr Holmes would not live to see you."

"What happened?" I inquired, while Mrs Hudson led me into the house.

"His heart, doctor, his heart," she sighed. "For several weeks now it has been ailing him, but in the past few days it has gotten worse. He had his first heat attack the day before yesterday. The doctor prescribed him some medicine and confined him to bed, but he still does not look well. He is pale and listless and does not eat."

I had guessed correctly.

"May I see him?"

"Yes of course, that is why I sent for you!" she said, tears forming in her eyes. Never had I seen her so wretched.

I quickly found my medical bag among my things and while the coachman unloaded the luggage Mrs Hudson and I entered the house.

As soon as I entered the vestibule I detected the unmistakable scent of Holmes's tobacco – which some might call a stench – and which I could never forget. The house was permeated with it just as our old lodgings had been. I recollected the times before we lived together when I would return from visiting him. My clothes had been so redolent with his tobacco that I immediately had to take them to be laundered.

Mrs Hudson, who knew me almost as well as she knew Holmes, wiped the tears from her face and opened the window in the vestibule.

"Mr Holmes does not like drafts; they are bad for his back. Now perhaps it will not bother him. Were he to roam about the house I would chase him back to bed with a broom until he recovered!"

"You ought to stop plying him with that sinfully rich food you cook so magnificently," said a voice above our heads, "and chase him immediately out into the sun so that he does not get in the way of your spring cleaning!"

From the stairway a large man in a black cloak and a bright white collar was descending with much huffing and puffing into the vestibule. Each step creaked under his weight and the banister groaned with the strain.

"You are right as always," conceded the housekeeper sadly. "This is Mr Barlow, who I told you about. And you must certainly know Dr Watson so well from Mr Holmes' tales that no introduction is necessary, isn't that right Pastor?"

"It is an honour to finally meet you," said Barlow, who having conquered the stairs was now shaking my hand vigorously. It glistened with sweat, just like his brow, the pate of his bald head and indeed his entire red face. It was difficult to say whether it was due to the heavy air in the house or some ailment.

Holmes had mentioned Barlow in one of his letters and I knew that he had recently become a frequent visitor at the house. Apparently this was due to their mutual fascination with philosophy and beekeeping. But now that I had the opportunity to scrutinise him, the jovial pastor's most conspicuous feature was not the baldness of his head, nor the corpulence of his body, nor the dampness of his skin, but a glass eye. Unmistakeably fixed in his left eye socket, with a pupil painted on a matte background, it gave him the distinct impression of squinting.

"Holmes finally fell asleep," said Barlow after we shook hands. "Sleep is good for him; I think that we ought to let him rest. What do you say, doctor, will you have a cup of tea with me meanwhile?"

His tone permitted no objection.

I would have preferred to immediately see my friend, and I must have subconsciously expressed this thought by frowning slightly, because the pastor put his arm around my shoulder and led me wordlessly into the drawing room. I did not prevent him. After all, regular rest is very important for patients with heart ailments.

The housekeeper hurried off to prepare some refreshments and Barlow and I reclined on a settee decorated with a hand-knitted throw rug made of Shetland wool. The pastor and I then spent more than an hour in friendly conversation over exquisite homemade apple cake and a pot of Ceylon tea, during which my opinion of him entirely altered. As unpleasant as my first impression of Barlow had been due to his appearance and devil's eye, during our conversation he proved to be an intelligent and eloquent companion. I was not surprised that he had become Holmes's friend.

"We first met last spring, when Mr Holmes developed a fascination with beekeeping," he recounted. "I have been raising bees at my parish for several years, naturally he came to me for advice."

"That is rather unusual for him."

"He was worried about his dear bees. It was the first time he had ever encountered the bee plague[7], which requires very

_____

[7] This disease is caused by the most dangerous bee mite *Varroa jacobsoni*. It's a creature 1.5 to 1.9 mm long, which preys on bee broods and lives on

sophisticated intervention. An amateur alone, even a talented one, stands no chance. But together we succeeded in finding a remedy!"

"He must have been grateful."

"My reward was finding a kindred spirit! In these parts one meets only farmers and peasants, who have little time for conversation or higher pursuits. At most you might see them in church on a Sunday. In Holmes I found someone with whom I could discuss much more than the cricket scores in the Eastbourne home league. No, Holmes was sent to me by the good Lord, and hopefully He will let him remain here a while longer."

"I hope so too," I said, gazing at the ceiling and glancing unwittingly at my pocket watch. It had been about twenty minutes since the last time I had checked it. The pastor correctly interpreted the gesture.

"I won't detain you further," he said smiling and wiping cake from his mouth. "I can see that you are eager to visit our patient. Perhaps he has gained strength enough to receive you. I believe that your visit will cheer him. We all hope that you will succeed in reviving him!"

It was most gracious of him to say so. I came to realise that this was indeed a man in his place. Though I reproached myself for not devoting enough time to my friend these past few years, I was relieved that my place at the side of the retired detective had been assumed by such a one as Barlow. I thanked him for his company, not only for those few moments that he

---

the bees after they hatch. Young bees that hatch from infected larvae suffer from various defects, such as lacking wings and legs, and soon die.

had devoted to me, but also for the months that he had spent with Holmes. Then I walked him to the doorstep.

Now it was time to see my old friend! I grabbed my medical bag, ran upstairs to the bedroom, knocked and entered immediately.

Sherlock Holmes was in a condition in which I had never seen him. He was asleep, lying motionless in bed, with the blanket pulled up over his chest. His wrinkled hands were resting alongside his body and his bony fingers dug into the bed sheet with each raspy intake of breath. His face, turned towards the window, through which a few rays of sunlight passed through half closed blinds, was ashen and sickly.

What a ruin my friend had become! The illness must have stricken him more powerfully than Mrs Hudson or Barlow, who saw him daily, suspected. I, who had not seen Holmes in a long time, was caught off-guard by his physical condition.

He turned his face to me, apparently because I had wakened him when I entered the bedroom. He strained to focus his gaze, but recognised me immediately, for he spoke to me through parched mouth.

"Examine me closely, my dear Watson," he said, coughing. "The body wastes away and slowly ceases to function. Regrettably the mind suffers even more, for it does not want to capitulate. Would you please give me some water?"

I did as he bade and sat down by the side of the bed.

"Nonsense, you look wonderful," I said, trying to placate him, but Holmes was not easily deceived. He drank greedily and I propped up his pillow on the brass headboard so that he could sit upright and speak more comfortably.

"If Mrs Hudson summoned you, my condition must be dire."

"Your deductions are misguided."

"Indeed? What else is one to think? My friend, who in the past year has only sent me a few letters, suddenly appears at my bedside wearing a funereal expression and carrying a medical bag. But I am glad to see you, Watson. Had I known that it would draw you out of your London burrow, I would have fallen ill sooner."

I ignored this gloomy talk and took my medical instruments out of the bag.

"When and how did your illness start?" I asked.

"Several weeks ago."

"Can you be more specific?"

"I felt the first faint paroxysm of lassitude at the end of March, but I put it down to seasonal weariness. Soon thereafter I began to suffer from shortness of breath, pains and heartburn."

"Why did you not inform me? I would have come immediately."

"My dear fellow," he said, smiling for the first time, "we are both of an age when we must expect these ailments. It would be strange indeed if nothing ailed us. And I did not anticipate that this minor affliction would worsen quite so quickly."

"Minor affliction? For God's sake, Holmes, you suffered a coronary! How can you be so flippant?"

"There is nothing else for it."

I sighed and placed my stethoscope on his chest. His heart was beating at an alarming rate. His breath was quick and strong, as though he had just run a race. His blood pressure also caused me concern; it was obvious that the danger was far from averted. I put away the Pinard horn and Holmes buttoned up his shirt.

"What medicines did they prescribe you?"

Holmes pointed to a jug of water and a tin filled with pills resting on the bedside table. Everything was what I would have prescribed.

"They are taking fine care of you," I said. "There is not much more that I can do now. Rest and take the medicines and you ought to feel better soon. I shall personally oversee your recovery."

The detective grew thoughtful.

"That will not please some people," he said mysteriously.

"What do you mean?"

"I haven't said a word to anyone yet, because I do not know whom I can trust. Besides Mrs Hudson, whom I did not want to frighten, you are the only one."

Then, in a conversational tone, as though he were assessing the quality of the roast, he leaned over to me and said: "I suspect that my heart ailment is no accident. I believe that I have been poisoned."

It was a moment before I understood the import of his words.

"Someone wants to kill you?" I cried. "Who? Why? How?"

"As yet I have no answers, but I presume that that package has something to do with it," he said, pointing with a tremulous finger at the wardrobe, on which lay a decorated ivory cigarette case.

"Your pipe tobacco?"

"Ironic, is it not? You always warned me of the dangers of smoking. It seems you were correct."

"I do not understand!"

"In the cigarette case you will find the last remains of some tobacco that I recently received as a gift. It is an exotic variety from India, about which even I knew nothing[8]. I was therefore unable to taste whether everything was as it should be. Nevertheless, the first signs of my *angina pectoris* appeared only after I began to smoke it. It certainly contains something that sapped my energy. It was some time before I connected the dots, but I did not have the opportunity to examine the tobacco, because the illness weakened me and confined me to bed. The rest you know."

"Who gave you the tobacco?"

"Pastor Barlow," said Holmes gloomily, closing his eyes for a moment.

Talking for long stretches evidently taxed him. He shook his head and rubbed the base of his beaklike nose drowsily. "I have not succeeded in piecing it together. Nevertheless, I do not think it was his intention and I believe he is unaware that he has become death's messenger."

Indeed the involvement of the good pastor in a conspiracy seemed farfetched, though I knew him but little and could not vouch for him.

"Why would someone want to kill you? You have not been working for years!"

---

[8] Holmes was an expert on tobacco and in the study of cigar ash. In 1879 he published a monograph entitled *Upon the Distinction Between the Ashes of the Various Tobaccos.*

"It is probably connected with a little puzzle that I have been asked to solve. The first request came around Christmas, and though I insisted that I would under no circumstances take on the investigation, after much persuasion I accepted. But then due to my health I was unable to undertake it. The letters are still in my desk."

"What was the case?"

"An Italian millionaire sought my advice. He suspected that someone wanted to kill him. He would only discuss the details in person and he asked me to come see him in order to uncover the menace and thwart it."

My thoughts raced as I tried to piece together the scattered bits of information.

"This Italian, what was his name?"

"Vito Minutti," said Holmes.

I rummaged feverishly through my bag, searching for the *Times*. I had already seen the name which Holmes had just uttered and I needed to confirm it. In a few seconds I confirmed that my memory was correct.

"Holmes, look!" I said, showing the detective the newspaper.

The detective read the first lines about Minutti's murder and turned even paler. His eyes widened and beads of sweat formed on his brow.

He finished reading and the paper fell from his limp hands to the floor.

"My God," he whispered. "Had I acted sooner I could have saved him!"

"You cannot prevent all the evil in the world, you cannot be everywhere at once," I said, trying to console him, but

Holmes no longer heard me. His blood pressure rose sharply and he grimaced as the pain shot through his left side.

It was bad.

I jumped up and began trying to bring him around.

"Mrs Hudson, come quick!" I shouted into the hallway. "Holmes is having another heart attack!"

II
A Funeral

The funeral of a legend is always a sad affair, especially for those who have spent a part of their lives or career with him. Pastor Barlow gave a eulogy for Sherlock Holmes in Fulworth church and many of the detective's friends attended. His brother Mycroft, a high-ranking government official, came from London together with Inspector Lestrade and several other police officers from Scotland Yard. I was especially touched and surprised to see the Countess Marie Framboise de Plessis-Bellie`re, with whom I had first become acquainted years ago during a certain infamous case in Bohemia. She must have been invited by Mrs Hudson, who had made a list of funeral guests according to my suggestions and from Holmes's address book.

After the eulogy the ceremony continued at the rustic local cemetery, under the vast blue sky. We gathered in a small open space near the oak coffin, the air smelling of elder and cut grass.

Watching Holmes's coffin slowly disappear into the earth was hard for all of us. Nobody tried to hide their tears. The words which Barlow uttered on behalf of the detective were no doubt beautiful and touching, but I do not remember any of them. In my head I was replaying everything that had happened in the last ten days, ever since I had received a telegram from Mrs Hudson about the dire state of my friend's health. The silence cut me off from the surrounding world with its merciful robe, giving me the opportunity to finally sort my agitated thoughts.

It started to rain. Umbrellas were pulled out and opened.

"If Holmes is looking at us from Heaven it must appear to him that black flowers are growing in his last resting place," said the Countess, grasping me by the arm.

At the funeral we all bade each other farewell. Nobody felt like sharing their mood with the others at dinner. Barlow accompanied us to the gates of the cemetery and scurried off to find shelter. Our London friends, including the Countess, made ready for their departure to the station to catch the afternoon train.

"Perhaps next time we will meet under happier circumstances," said the Countess, squeezing my hand as Mycroft helped her into the carriage.

"I fear that we will never get over this loss," said Lestrade.

Mycroft and I exchanged silent glances and left his remark unanswered. The spring storm and wind scattered us, the carriage disappeared behind the trees and I took a hansom back to Cuckmere Haven, the rain drumming on the canvas roof.

Mrs Hudson, who had not attended the funeral, already had food prepared. While she set the table and chased flies out of the dining room I stepped into Holmes's bedroom.

The detective was standing at the window with his hands behind his back, listening to the howling of the wind between the casements. He did not so much as glance in my direction when I greeted him.

"I trust that you buried me with all honours," he said, his gaze fixed on the glistening leaves in the garden.

"You and your charades. Are you aware that the Countess Framboise was in attendance? It almost broke her heart. I presume that you are enjoying yourself?"

"No indeed, Watson. My enemies have already buried me so many times that I fear no one will notice when I finally do pass on. I will personally visit the Countess once this matter has been resolved."

"Enemies?" I cried. "You have arranged most of your funerals yourself!"

"But only in order to confuse the criminal element and take advantage of their reduced vigilance. But this time it is different, my friend. This time it is personal."

The last time I had seen Holmes express such hatred was after the death of Professor Moriarty. Back then he had disappeared and been considered dead for three years.

In his retirement Holmes never would have anticipated such an attack, and if the murderer had been provoked merely by the request of the deceased Minutti, something big must have been afoot. For this reason the detective decided to "succumb" to the poison that was hidden in the tobacco and arranged his funeral so that his unknown enemy would lower his defences.

Only I, Mrs Hudson and Mycroft knew the truth.

For several days Holmes lay concealed and recovered under my careful watch. In less than two weeks I managed to restore his blood pressure and heart rhythm to normal. I adjusted his regimen so that he would gain strength and return to the world of the living.

Today was his first day out of bed, and while I participated in the tasteless theatre for the outside world, he conducted an analysis of the poisoned tobacco.

"My suspicion has been confirmed, it indeed contains traces of *digitalis*," he said dryly. "Somebody wanted to prepare a sweet death for me."

"It was ingeniously planned," I said, nodding.

Like every man of medicine I was well acquainted with the *digitalis* plant family, and I had to concede that mixing the dried leaves into Holmes's tobacco was brilliant. Except for a slight sweetness the herb is practically tasteless. The symptoms which the detective suffered also suggested its use: headaches, lack of appetite and irregular pulse. From my medical practice I knew of cases where people had made tea out of *digitalis*, mistaking it for the harmless *comphrey*, or children who had been poisoned by drinking water from a vase containing the plant. Fortunately Holmes's murderer had endeavoured to use subtlety and had prepared the deadly tobacco in such a small concentration that my friend's heart was only gradually weakened.

Thus Holmes had succeeded in uncovering the plan at the last moment.

"We have confirmed how," I said. "Now all that remains is to determine who and why."

"Yes, I admit that I am overwhelmed with curiosity," said Holmes, rubbing his chin. "Well then, we might as well start with our dear Barlow."

"But there is one more thing..."

"Which is?"

"Who will conduct the investigation? You are officially dead and cannot appear in public. And I can hardly catch the murderer by myself."

"My dear fellow!" laughed Holmes. "It is but a trifle!"

***

The next morning, a certain Mr Cedric Parker of Stone Terrace, Weston-Super-Mare appeared in the vestibule of Holmes's house. The detective had selected the identity of his cousin, coming to arrange his estate, as the ideal disguise to assist him in moving freely and inconspicuously during the investigation without being disclosed.

He had not shaved for several days and he trimmed his full beard into an elegant grey-flecked point. He stopped brushing his hair straight back and instead parted it to the right and smoothed it with brilliantine. He left the greying in his temples, but coloured his eyebrows in order to give his face a different expression. He also donned round spectacles with transparent glass. His attire consisted of a summer suit with a vest, which was quite a contrast to his usual rather homely clothes. Taking into account the family resemblance, which nobody would think twice about, an entirely different person now stood before me.

"Holmes, I do not recognise you!"

"Then I am satisfied," said the detective, studying his new appearance in the mirror. "But I still do not much resemble the real Cedric. Let us hope that no one takes it into their head to look for his photograph."

"This cousin of yours really exists?" I asked. "I thought you had invented him! You never mentioned him before!"

"Indeed, Cedric Edward Parker is an actual member of my extended family[9]. I wanted to give my alter ego a certain

---

[9] Sherlock Holmes was the son of Siger Holmes and Violet Sherrinford, the youngest of the three daughters of Sir Edward Sherrinford. We can assume that Cedric Edward Parker was the son of one of the elder of the two Sherrinford daughters.

measure of credibility in case Barlow or any other curious soul decided to confirm my family circumstances at the register office. One can never be too cautious."

Once Mrs Hudson had approved the detective's disguise we were finally ready to attempt a dress rehearsal. It was time to pay a visit to Pastor Barlow and untangle the circumstances of his role in the unsuccessful attempt on Holmes's life.

We walked out into the front yard, where Holmes again felt the sunshine on his face after so many days confined to the house. He paused for a moment, spread his arms and inhaled deeply.

"It was rather tiresome staying indoors so long," he said. "But for a dead man I feel wonderful!"

I admonished him for this blasphemy and headed to the coach, but Holmes stopped me.

"Better to walk," he said. "The exercise will do me good and it will be excellent if people see me. I don't have anything to hide."

I agreed and followed the detective. We left the estate and headed to the pastor's farmstead along the dusty path by the south slope of the local coastline with its magnificent view of the Channel. Beneath us cliffs extended to the pebbly beach below, from where we could hear the cries of seagulls.

We walked through the outskirts of the town, bidding good day to several villagers, and even passed by the cemetery, where Holmes took a morbid delight in his grave. The flowers that people had brought and which practically covered the gravestone gave him pause, but the expression in his eyes was neither sad nor regretful, but shone with satisfaction.

People had come from near and far to pay tribute to the greatest of detectives, a legend in the battle against crime and injustice, who helped everyone regardless of their station.

"They have buried me a hundred times, and a hundred times I have risen," said Holmes. "As long as there is crime in the world I will continue to rise."

"We could not hope for more," I added.

Talking thus we arrived at Barlow's rectory.

Everything indicated that the pastor was at home; but not alone, as we deduced from the automobile parked before the gate to his house, a magnificent Silver Ghost that shone in the sunlight. Local children were gathered about the car with reverent expressions on their faces.

"We have come at an inconvenient time," I said. "Perhaps we should return later. We could come for afternoon tea."

But Holmes appeared not to be listening. His attention was completely captivated by the Rolls Royce with its elegant open silver body and black seats. For a moment he was like one of these small rogues as he admired the luxurious vehicle. In those days automobiles were already becoming a relatively common sight in the city, but in the countryside they attracted much attention.

"Have you never seen an automobile?" I teased.

"Of course I have," he answered, without tearing his eyes from the Silver Ghost. "But one does not often come across such a beautiful specimen, my friend. This is the best car in the world. It won the gold medal in the Scottish Reliability Trial for its speed and handling. It also set the world record for driving without stopping. Imagine: it travelled without stopping a total

25

of twenty-seven times the distance from Glasgow to London, or some fifteen thousand miles!"

"You sound like a brochure, Holmes. I suppose you will also tell me how much it costs."

"Upwards of three thousand pounds," he said. "I briefly considered buying one, but for an old man such as I it would be a pure extravagance."

Now I recognised the old Holmes. His ascetic nature had overcome his enchantment.

Suddenly the door of the parish burst open and out shot Barlow's visitor. He shooed away the cluster of children around his automobile and with a contemptuous glance silently climbed behind the wheel and started the engine.

"Good upbringing can't be bought," said Holmes loudly.

The man looked around and realised that the comment was directed at him.

"Mind your own business!" he shouted at us, donning his driving gloves and slipping a pair of goggles over his bulbous nose and large moustache. Glowering at us from beneath bushy eyebrows, he honked loudly on the claxon and sped off, leaving a band of shouting children in his wake. He was an unpleasant person with whom I did not wish to have further intercourse.

The commotion also brought Barlow outside.

"Dr Watson!" he cried when he saw me on the driveway. "I did not expect to see you here today! To what do I owe the pleasure?"

Judging by the expression on his face, however, I doubted that he was in fact pleased to see me. He looked like a schoolboy who had been caught cheating.

"Mr Cedric Parker, Holmes's cousin, has arrived in order to arrange the detective's estate," I said, introducing my companion to the fat pastor. "It occurred to me that I should pay you a visit and use the opportunity to show Cedric the country where our friend lived happily for so long."

The two men shook hands. I was numb with suspense as to whether Barlow might see through Holmes's disguise, and those few seconds when he examined Parker seemed like an eternity. Fortunately, the pastor did not evince even the slightest suspicion. Holmes's cousin apparently did not warrant so much as a second glance.

"Certainly, gentlemen, please be my guests," he said nodding to the door with his eyes fixed on the departing automobile. "In a moment my housekeeper will have tea ready. Will you stay?"

"Gladly," said Holmes. "I hope that we did not interrupt your visitor. The gentleman seemed rather upset."

"Oh, you need not worry about him, he is one of my parishioners," the pastor mumbled while leading us inside. "He brought a donation for our parish, which I will use to finance repairs to the roof of the church."

The man did not look like someone who was kept awake at night by concern about the sanctuary of Fulworth's believers nor did the pastor seem to want to talk about him. Holmes's curiosity was supremely piqued, but he said nothing, of course, to avoid angering our host.

Indeed, a cheque was lying on the vestibule table, the ink still wet. I tried to make out the name of the donor and the amount, but Barlow tossed a newspaper and several letters onto the table.

He led us into the garden and to a sunny gazebo where the housekeeper had laid out tea, or rather what resembled an early luncheon. Judging by the size of the repast, it was difficult to imagine what the pastor's actual luncheon might be.

So far each meeting that I had had with this man, with the exception of the funeral, had featured a culinary accompaniment of various proportions. He ate food as others breathe air. For every morsel that I swallowed Barlow inhaled four and by and by all that remained of the chicken on his plate were a few bones. No wonder he was so fat! If as yet he suffered no ill effects, I predicted he would in the near future.

"If I could not eat a fine meal which of life's joys would remain to me?" he said. "I have no wife, my life belongs to God, and I need hardly mention other vices. Take our dear friend Holmes, the same age as I am, who ate rather poorly his whole life, and who is now with God while we sit here and talk. I think that my health is in the best of hands!"

He crossed himself and poured a cup of black coffee.

"Holmes clearly had a bad doctor," said Holmes, screwing up his face.

I shot him a glance, but the pastor, digesting contentedly, spiritedly defended me.

"Dr Watson did everything in his power! Unfortunately, Holmes was beyond help. He paid for his genius with his weaknesses and excessive strains."

"Weaknesses? Do you mean smoking?"

"Certainly."

"You are right," I said. "Unfortunately, we all encouraged him in this vice. Indeed, you recently brought him some valuable tobacco, I believe from India..."

Barlow clearly did not realise that Holmes had related this to me before his death.

"Oh, that is true," he admitted with a wry smile and, it seemed to me, perspiring even more than usual. "Do not be cross with me. I too received it as a gift, but I do not smoke. I did not know anyone else who would appreciate it more than Sherlock, which is why I gave it to him."

"I do not mean to take issue with you," I clarified. "In fact, Holmes valued your friendship greatly and told me about the tobacco only in connection with the gratitude that he felt towards you as a friend."

A blush appeared on the pastor's baroque face and he blinked humbly. In the sunlit garden, among the blooming rhododendrons and singing birds, he seemed almost saintly. How could he have been involved in the plot to kill Holmes?

The detective coughed, put down his cup of coffee and wiped his mouth with a napkin.

"I still have not seen today's paper. Have they written anything about Sherlock's funeral?"

"Would you believe it, I do not know myself!" said Barlow jumping out of his chair. "I shall fetch the paper this instant!"

He hurried off and a moment later returned with the paper. He spread the local daily before us, which was full of articles about Sherlock Holmes. Although I had not seen a reporter at the funeral, several columns of newsprint were devoted to the memorial service and the ceremony.

"I regret that I was not able to attend," said the detective.

I smiled inwardly. He sincerely meant it, not as Parker, but as Holmes.

"It was a beautiful ceremony," said Barlow. "Most dignified and touching."

The detective raised his head and I saw his chin twitch.

"Would you excuse me for a moment?" he asked the pastor, his voice trembling.

"Yes, of course," said the pastor. "May I be of any assistance?"

Holmes turned his head away, clenching the newspaper.

"No, I just need to be alone for a minute," he said quietly and left through the garden to the vestibule.

No doubt this was a rehearsed performance and I was relieved to see that it had impressed Barlow.

"Mr Parker must be a very sensitive man; the death of our friend has distressed him greatly," he said, leaning back in his armchair and biting into the dessert with relish.

"He was recalling the memory of their childhood together," I said. "He will be all right."

Thankfully Barlow was sitting with his back to the house and I could watch through the French windows as Holmes snuck into the pastor's ground floor office and began rummaging through his desk.

While I watched in horror lest our host turn around or lest Holmes be caught by the housekeeper, I tried to continue the conversation in a casual tone. The detective went through the office with his usual attention to detail; he did not leave one drawer, bookshelf or closet unsearched, though he took care to not leave any traces that he had been there.

The pastor turned around to look for Mr Parker just as the detective was returning. He brought back the newspaper which he had taken with him in his fit of distress.

We lingered for another hour or so conversing politely and then bade the pastor farewell.

We returned home on foot, along the same path past the coast and cemetery.

"I am at somewhat of a loss, Watson," said Holmes, when I asked him whether he had found anything out of the ordinary in Barlow's study. "What I saw at the good pastor's house has raised more questions than furnished answers."

"What do you mean?"

"The first thing that caught my eye was the pastor's reaction when he realised that we had seen his previous visitor. Did you see how he grew pale?"

"Indeed, he was not pleased when we mentioned it."

"I must find out this gentleman's name," said Holmes.

"That will not be easy. Barlow will certainly not tell us. Perhaps we could find out by means of the automobile; surely there will not be many of them driving around Surrey!"

"A capital idea, my friend!" said Holmes. "It had occurred to me as well, but I have devised another way to find out more quickly."

With these words he removed the front page of Barlow's newspaper from his breast pocket. Apparently he had torn it away when he had disappeared with it into the pastor's study. "As always, when I need to know something I can consult the daily paper!"

"Is there an article in it about that man?" I inquired.

"Certainly not, but the paper hides the answer we seek," said the detective smiling. "The ink on the cheque over which the pastor placed this newspaper was wet. You see, the outlines of letters are visible!"

31

I studied the paper in the places that Holmes indicated. Though practically illegible, in several places you could nevertheless trace the mirrored print of the signature on the cheque and the amount.

"With a magnifying glass, a good light and a little bit of luck we will be able to decipher the signature!"

"So that is why you contrived to enter the house!"

"Yes, and to search Barlow's study. I had already been in it several times, but always just for a short while, and I had no reason to search it until today. Several things surprised me."

As usual he kept me in suspense before revealing his findings, but this time I did not urge him. I waited until he spoke, which presently he did.

"The queerest thing was his bookshelf. Barlow has an impressive collection of books and publications about beekeeping, but all of them are brand new. Untouched, unread, and judging by the dust on the shelves, unused. In the desk drawers I also found a bill for a new bee colony, which he ordered about a year ago. It seems that before that he did not have any at all!"

I realised what he was insinuating.

"Nevertheless, he always presented himself as a passionate beekeeper with years of experience. He also helped me resolve a great many problems."

"Yes, he told me," I said.

"But now that I think about it, I have never actually seen him in direct contact with bees. I always took his advice, and it always proved sound!"

By the end of the journey Holmes and I had come to the conclusion that the pastor could only have received the advice from a third person and had been merely dissimulating a love of bees. This, of course, could only mean one thing: his friendship with Holmes had been a calculated move. As unpleasant and painful as this thought was, the detective had no doubt.

"It grieves me, but I have encountered far stranger things," Holmes said coldly. "It reminds me that in this world I can trust only you and my brother."

Indeed, that evening Mycroft Holmes, about whom the detective spoke so affectionately, sent us a telegram that tested at least one part of this assertion.

III
The Letter Written in Blue Blood

In the letter, which arrived in the afternoon mail, Mycroft insisted that Holmes come to London post-haste. It was impossible to leave that same day, so the detective asked Mrs Hudson to reserve a place on the morning train. He carelessly tossed aside the telegram, saying that he would devote the rest of the evening to examining the letters on the cheque imprint.

While my imagination and curiosity ran wild and I ruminated about what could have prompted the usually reserved Mycroft to write such a feverish telegram, Holmes withdrew and calmly studied the markings and lines of the ink print.

"Are you not even the least bit interested why he wants to see us?" I asked.

"There is doubtlessly a compelling reason, one that involves the search for my killer. I could pace nervously until tomorrow, but that would be to no purpose. I prefer to focus on matters of significance."

He returned to his work and did not raise his head again until well into the night. I let him be and picked up a book, which I scarcely read. Instead I reviewed the events of the day. I had no doubt that Holmes would get even with the treacherous priest, but now it was imperative that we not frighten him off. One clue was the cheque and the signature of the unknown man, whose involvement in the plot we so far only suspected. Could the cheque have been payment for delivering the deadly tobacco?

Holmes finished his analysis only after midnight. Waverley[10] had just conquered Edinburgh, and his adventures had successfully helped me ward off sleep.

I knew that his work was finished when he set aside the magnifying glass, stretched out and cracked his knuckles. I hated that sound, but he did it unwittingly.

"Did you find what you expected?"

"Only partially."

He switched off his desk lamp and brought a piece of paper covered in writing to the light of the fire. On it he had copied the lines of the ink print from the pastor's newspaper in order to decipher the signature.

"The first thing that I discovered, under the assumption that the cheque was indeed a payment for Barlow's services, is that the market price for my death is two thousand pounds," said the detective. "That is a rather handsome sum for a retired beekeeper, wouldn't you say? Some of my contemporaries do not command even a fraction of this price."

I did not find his dark humour amusing, but he cackled with delight.

"As for the rest, the results are inconclusive."

"You were unable to determine the name?"

"Not entirely, though I have narrowed the possibilities. The ink print is of poor quality. I dare say, however, that the man's first name is Robert or Rupert. Do you see, the first letter *R* is visible, and the second letter must be either *o* or *u*."

He showed me the paper on which he had examined and connected the lines.

---

[10] *Waverley* (1814), by Sir Walter Scott (1771–1832).

"The third letter is illegible, but is clearly followed by an *e*. The last two letters are without doubt *r* and *t*. Alas, it is impossible to decipher more of the first name."

Indeed, the rest was only some illegible squiggles.

"On the other hand, I am certain that the initial of his middle name is *H*," Holmes continued. "The surname then starts with the letter *D*, the next several letters are unclear, and the last four letters are without a doubt *ford*."

"At least this can lead us in the right direction."

"Certainly. Another clue is that luxurious automobile. Perhaps I can deduct even more from the letters, though of course only trifles."

"What else besides the man's name can be determined?"

"My dear fellow, I see that you are unfamiliar with the field of graphology! I need hardly be surprised, however; from the empirical perspective it is considered a highly hypothetical discipline. Nevertheless, despite being reproached for its unscientific method, it has many proponents."

"I am not qualified to judge," I said, shaking my head. "I only have the most superficial knowledge of it."

"Well then, you know that graphology is a branch of psychology that focuses on the study of handwriting and its relationship to human behaviour. It is based on the assumption that it is impossible to find any two people who have exactly the same handwriting. Handwriting is unique, and according to graphologists, expresses the human personality."

As a doctor, this naturally interested me. Until then I had assumed that graphology was simply a method for determining the authenticity of signatures. I had no idea it could conceal such information.

"The size of the letters corresponds to the author's status and self-confidence," said Holmes, explaining that the foundations of the theory had been laid by Aristotle himself. "Larger letters belong to important authors, smaller ones to those who are cautious. Very small letters are written by people who are timid and have low self-confidence. Larger letters, about four millimetres, belong to people who have a sense of detail. They are critical, practical and realistic. Large letters are used by those who are dynamic and have a healthy sense of self-confidence; they tend to be optimistic and magnanimous. Our man has a tendency to be wasteful and one-dimensional. Overly large letters testify to a loss of self-control. But as you yourself can certainly concede, these are not very demonstrable conclusions."

"Nevertheless, it is fascinating what just a few letters can suggest!" I said.

"Indeed," the detective nodded. "Except that a larger sample is required for a truly precise evaluation; we would need at least a page of written text. One examines the overall structure of the written text, the pressure of the pen, the size of the letters, their width, slant, spaces between words, distance and direction of the lines and many other factors. The age and gender of the writer also play a role as does whether he is right- or left-handed. From what I have available and from our cursory meeting with this person, I can gather only very little. In my opinion, we are dealing with a maniac."

Thus Holmes closed the investigation for the evening and went to his room. Barlow, the mysterious guest, the failed murder attempt and Mycroft's letter would all have to wait until the morning.

***

The fresh wind from the Thames welcomed us to London with its embrace shortly after Big Ben struck noon. Holmes and I stood on the northern embankment in front of Westminster Palace[11] at the entrance of peers, he in his disguise and I in my best suit. After all, it was not every day that I visited Great Britain's house of parliament, and I regarded Mycroft's invitation as a great honour.

I had always had an odd and somewhat personal relationship to the parliament building. After the tragic fire on October 16, 1834, when most of the palace had been destroyed, my uncle had become a member of the committee in charge of its reconstruction. Only Westminster Hall, the Jewel Tower, and the crypt in the chapel of St. Stephen were spared. The committee then selected from among some hundred designs, and the foundation stone for the reconstruction of the palace in the neo-gothic style was placed in 1840, on the day when my parents met.

Mycroft's office was in this building. Although I never learned exactly what position he occupied in the government hierarchy, it must have been very important and in some way connected with state security. Holmes once even mentioned something about the secret service.

---

[11] Westminster Palace, now the seat of the Parliament of Great Britain, dates from the year 1097 and is the oldest preserved part of Westminster Hall. The palace served until the 16th century as the residence of the monarch. Most of the present building dates from the 19th century, when the palace was reconstructed after a devastating fire.

We did not wait for him long; Mycroft met us at the entrance exactly at the agreed time. He greeted us quickly with a nod of his head, and as was his habit, did not waste time with common pleasantries. He immediately led us into the palace, where we were searched by an officer of the metropolitan police. Neither I nor Holmes protested; it had long been an obligation of every British citizen who entered the building.

The most famous attempt to disrupt the palace was the Gunpowder Plot in 1605, in which Catholic extremists attempted to detonate a charge of gunpowder during the opening ceremonies of the sitting of parliament. The conspiracy was uncovered after one of the Catholic nobles received an anonymous warning not to participate in the celebrations. The palace administration launched a search and discovered the charge and one of the conspirators, Guy Fawkes. The participants in the conspiracy were sentenced to death in Westminster Hall.

The original palace was also the site of an attempt on the life of Prime Minister Spencer Perceval in 1812. When he left the members' lobby of the Lower House, he was attacked and shot by John Bellingham. Perceval is the only British prime minister to have been assassinated.

All of this was running through my head as the parliament staff dressed in knee breeches, stockings and coats with starched collars were graciously dismissed from Mycroft's personal security and we walked to his office on the top floor.

We made our way though corridors lined with enormous bookshelves and paintings of famous figures, passed through rooms in which history was being written and ascended staircases, of which there were perhaps a hundred in the whole

39

gigantic palace. Indeed, the building has more than a thousand rooms and several kilometres of hallways!

Finally we arrived in the third floor office, where Mycroft bade us sit on a comfortable leather sofa, poured us sherry and offered us cigars.

"Not for me, the last one almost killed me," said Holmes.

Mycroft snapped shut the mahogany case and transferred his burly frame to the desk.

"Gentlemen, allow me to get straight to the matter," he said dramatically.

Long introductions were not among his habits. He was a man of action.

"I have called you here on a matter of utmost national importance!"

"I would not expect you to rouse me from the grave for anything less," said Holmes.

"Yes, I know that you are officially dead and are engaged in the pursuit of your killer," said Mycroft. "It is indeed this fact that can ensure the necessary discretion in this sensitive matter, and perhaps even has something in common with your case."

The official opened a drawer in his desk, took out a thick paper envelope and placed it on the writing pad. For a moment he played with its edges indecisively, but then he opened it, not for the first time judging from its broken seal, and took out a letter written on handmade paper and passed it across the desk to Holmes.

"This letter was waiting for me when I returned from Fulworth three days ago."

The detective began devouring the lines, but the contents for now remained hidden from me. The only thing that I noticed with astonishment was the personal seal of King George![12]

"Was it written by who I think?" I asked.

Mycroft did not reply. He only lit a cigar and silently released clouds of pungent smoke to the ceiling while Holmes read.

"Fascinating," said Holmes when he had finished reading the mysterious letter.

His misanthropic elder brother nodded seriously and fell to thinking.

It vexed me that I was the only one in the room who still did not know what was afoot. I coughed with embarrassment and shot an inquisitive glance at my friend.

"Excuse me, doctor," said Mycroft, "we do not want to keep you in the dark. We first have to clarify what precisely is going on. The letter is indeed from His Majesty. It is a request to the secret service for help. He wants to find his nephew, Lord Bollinger, who recently vanished without a trace."

"Bollinger... that name means something to me," I said, searching my memory.

"Albert Bollinger is *de facto* the King's foster nephew," said Holmes. "He is the son of Queen Mary's brother. We met him once briefly."

Now I remembered meeting this man. He had then been still very young, with handsome and noble features, remotely resembling his aunt with her piercing brown eyes, oval face and

---

[12] George V (1865 –1936), who ruled from 1910–1936. He continued the anti-German stance of his father Edward VII. Although under his reign Great Britain won the First World War, the Empire emerged greatly weakened.

pointy chin. Today he must have been over thirty. Years before I had spoken with him at a court reception, one of the few to which Holmes had accepted an invitation.

"But I still do not understand why his disappearance, though lamentable, should be investigated by the secret service and not the police," I said. "And what makes you think it is connected with the attempt on Sherlock's life?"

Mycroft became even gloomier and the corners of his mouth drooped.

"Lord Bollinger and his family own industrial enterprises in northern England. I need not emphasise that these include important munitions factories. After the destructive fire in Curry, the factory in Manchester has been our most vital one for half a year. Bollinger is someone whom His Majesty regularly consults regarding research and development. The King has even entrusted him with drafting secret strategic documents for protecting the country if the tension between us and Emperor Wilhelm[13] escalates into war."

"What types of documents are they?" asked Holmes.

---

[13] Wilhelm II of the Hohenzollern dynasty (1859 – 1941), who from 1888 – 1918 was German Emperor and King of Prussia. He ascended the throne at the age of 29 after the 99-day reign of his father Frederick III. He stirred international controversy by his uncompromising attitude to the building of the German fleet, which the UK perceived as an attack on its naval hegemony. English efforts to improve relations with Germany foundered. Wilhelm generously supported the army, which under his rule became the largest and best equipped in the world. From the moment he came to the throne he did not hide his warlike ambitions and was undoubtedly one of the architects of the First World War. After his overthrow during the November Revolution of 1918 he fled to the Netherlands.

"Designs for new types of weapons, war machines and everything connected with them," said Mycroft. "Then there is tactical information and deployment plans for our armed forces."

"Now I understand why the King is so concerned with his disappearance and why you see a clear connection between our two cases," said the detective, returning the letter.

The connection was now becoming evident to me too.

Holmes's brother had connected Bollinger's disappearance with the death of Italian factory owner Minutti, whose letter, sent just before his death, had apparently provoked the attempt on the detective's life. Both men had been, and we hoped the King's nephew still was, renowned industrialists and among the main developers and manufacturers of arms.

"Something bad is happening exceeding all borders," said Mycroft, summing up our thoughts. "We all know how the international situation is becoming more complicated. These connected disappearances or deaths of people directly or indirectly responsible for the defensive capabilities of nations do not bode well. In our case, I would be willing to concede that Bollinger was captured by the German secret service, but Italy is neutral, at least for the time being. Germany hopes that she will become her ally and Minutti's death does not fit. There is no logic or order, which is what terrifies me most!"

"What do you need me to do?" asked Holmes.

The official extinguished his cigar and folded his arms.

"Your task is to confirm the connection between Bollinger's disappearance, Minutti's death and the attack on you," said Mycroft gravely. "You must determine who has an interest in threatening the European arms industry and if possible thwart the plot."

43

"To investigate Minutti's murder I will have to visit Italy," said the detective. "Can I count on the government's support?"

"I am afraid not," said Mycroft shaking his head. "Germany could consider any official activity on the territory of its neighbour and potential ally as a provocation. If you have any problems, the Ministry will not get involved."

"How ideal," said Holmes, rising from the sofa.

I rose too. We were ready to depart.

"Do not be sarcastic," his brother rebuked. "Your country does not deserve it."

"I was not being sarcastic," said the detective, smiling. "On the contrary, the fact that no officials or policeman will interfere greatly increases my chances of solving the case."

"Then you accept the assignment?"

Holmes slapped his brother on his pudgy shoulder.

"Let no one say that I turned my back on my country."

For the first time since I had known him, Mycroft smiled.

"Nobody would dare," he said. "One does not speak ill of the dead."

IV
Behind the Walls of San Michele

We did not return to Fulworth the evening after visiting Mycroft. All of the local clues were known to us and we did not want Barlow to suspect anything. Holmes only asked his brother to have the police watch the parish and the pastor's movements during our absence and provide us with regular reports.

The next task that the detective entrusted to Mycroft's security unit was to contact Rolls-Royce in Manchester to obtain a list of Silver Ghost owners. We hoped by means of the key letters to obtain the name of the man to whom Barlow had written the cheque. Under normal circumstances he would of course have taken this step himself, but time was of the essence. With perhaps a hint of optimism he hoped that the police could handle this relatively simple task.

We spent another day and a half in London making preparations for our journey, quickly so as not to lose the trail.

Holmes and I had been to Venice before, but this watery city, cleft by hundreds of narrow canals, never ceased to enchant and astonish me. Clamorous modern Italy here met the poignant and romantic beauty of ancient palaces, intensified by the reflected September light in the twilight. When we arrived the omnipresent water was dotted with boats, *vaporettos* and gondolas. Minutti lived here with his family, because most of his companies were scattered across northern Italy.

On the journey the detective studied Mycroft's files. They contained information about Minutti and Lord Bollinger, their habits, families and friends, and if such were known by the secret service, rumours about their affairs and perversions. It was up to Holmes to determine what information was important and could contain a clue about what to do next.

The evening after our arrival we took rooms in the Regina Hotel near the Santa Lucia station, tired after our long journey. We went straight to bed without even taking supper, as though we knew that this night would be the last for a long time when we could sleep in peace.

We were awoken by the sound of Italy; the unmistakable jumble of street noises, shouting, heckling and spirited conversations in the street under the window; a din that only the citizens of this sunny and excitable country could make. We ate a light breakfast and headed off for the city, to a meeting without which the investigation could not get underway.

Since we had risen early we did not have to hurry. I was tempted to pass through the Grand Canal, the main Venetian boat thoroughfare, but Holmes insisted that we go by foot. He was in good spirits after his years spent in the country. He liked this way of life and was impressed by the light-heartedness and speed of everything here. Vessels darted through the water as people travelled to work or from the markets, past petty verbal exchanges between gondoliers and people swarming the narrow sidewalks that weave through Venice and smack of quaint odours.

We crossed what seemed like a hundred bridges before we arrived at our destination: St. Mark's Square. Holmes selected a table in front of one of the cafés that had a fine view of the basilica and its tall bell tower.

He settled into a chair and ordered a cup of coffee.

"How beautiful, but to reside here longer than a few weeks would drive one to madness," he said, stretching his body. "I am glad to see that the bell tower is almost rebuilt."

The detective was alluding to the last time we had been in Venice, in the case of the Doge's diamond in 1901, only a short time before the five hundred year old tower had collapsed, the result of a fire long ago. No doubt fire was the plague of civilisation in the nineteenth century. It was a miracle that nobody had been harmed. The only victim of the falling building was the caretaker's cat.

I was jolted back into the present by the brisk footsteps of a swarthy gentleman with a cane. He approached Holmes, leaned on his cane and looked in the same direction in which Holmes fixed his gaze.

"A morning such as this is practically invitations one to chat over a cup of coffee," said the man, his eyes fixed on the basilica. "May I recommend that you give the band a few coins to play a folk song?"

Without so much as glancing at the man, the detective wiped his lips with his napkin and winked at me.

"Do you have a particular song in mind?"

"How about *La tabaccheria mia*?"

"Thank you, but I prefer to delight in the beauty of the city in silence," Holmes replied. "Please, sit with us."

Mycroft had devised the code especially for this case. The secret service frequently used call and response so that people who had never met could identify one another. This was doubly important for Holmes, who was travelling under the name of his cousin Cedric[14].

"Welcome to Venice, my friends," said the man and he promptly sat down at our table.

"Thank you, Mr ..."

"No last names, please. Just call me Paolo."

He pulled out from his breast pocket a packet of folded documents and handed them to Holmes. The detective began to unfold them, but the man stopped him. He held Holmes's hand under the table and looked around the square to see if we were being watched.

"Wait until I leave," he said. "You can never be too careful. This is a sensitive case, and if it was discovered that I have spoken to you, I would be in danger."

"What have you given me?"

"What your London office requested. Records from the investigation of the death of Signor Minutti. These are copies of all the important documents and my notes. Judge for yourself."

"Excellent. If I need anything else, how do I find you?"

The Italian agent discretely gave us another document.

"I am at your service. Here are instructions for using the drop off point."

We assured him that we would use it only when absolutely necessary. Paolo once again scanned the square and then disappeared into the crowd. Everything had happened so fast that it seemed like a dream.

As soon as he was gone, Holmes began hungrily examining the documents.

---

[14] One can read about Holmes's family in *Sherlock Holmes of Baker Street: A life of the world's first consulting detective* by William S. Baring-Gould.

"Let's take a look," he muttered. "Evidently, the *carabinieri* have not given the investigation the attention one would expect in the murder of such an important person."

"How so?"

"Minutti was killed almost three weeks ago, but so far they have failed to find anything. Everything suggests that the case was simply set aside. Minutti was shot, but the police were unable to find anyone who had heard anything. His office is easily accessible and anyone could get in when the secretary was at lunch; but none of the hundreds of employees has testified that they noticed anything or anyone out of the ordinary. What's more, everyone has an alibi. There are no fingerprints or footprints at the scene of the crime, nothing at all. The perpetrator's motive is also unknown. Minutti was rather well-liked."

"But there must be a bullet," I said.

"It was never found," said Holmes. "Neither in the room nor in the body."

"Strange."

"Indeed. Nevertheless, the body has been returned to the family and was buried last week in the San Michele cemetery. In this way the opportunity to find other clues on the body of the victim has been all but eliminated."

He finished reading the document and began focussing on Paolo's notes.

"According to the findings of our mysterious friends, this is not just a matter of police incompetence, but a much more dangerous game involving people in high places. Apparently the authorities were not interested in shedding light on the incident.

Paolo's source even asserts that a small bribe was paid to one of the commissars!"

"Outrageous!"

"But effective. The chances of finding the murderer are now practically *nil*."

"If we found the recipient of the bribe it would lead us to the murderer."

"There is no evidence of the bribe; it is merely a suspicion. We do not even know who was meant to be its recipient. There are many in the local criminal hierarchy who are capable of thwarting an investigation. What's more, I fear that the police will cover each other's backs, just as they do everywhere else in the world, even in England. That is probably why Paolo thinks he is in danger."

"What about Minutti's family? They have a great deal of influence. Are they not following the investigation?"

"The poor wretch left behind only a widow and her thoughts after this tragic loss are somewhere else entirely," sighed Holmes. "I am not surprised that our friend was so careful."

"Have we reached an impasse?"

"I wouldn't call it that. I would say merely that should you ever write a literary account of this case, as is your wont, a short story will not suffice."

The hot Italian sun compelled us to seek the shade of the hotel. Holmes retired for a while to his room to organise his thoughts. Someone had apparently tried to sever the threads that would unknot this thorny case, but enough of them still remained for us to continue.

Directly after lunch the detective set off in pursuit of one of them.

We hired a boat and a rower and set off into the restless waters of the Grand Canal. My friend was perched in the bow of the craft, his eyes roving and watching the events around us like a hawk. The fish and vegetable markets had just closed, lackeys were loading empty crates and leftover goods and sprayed the paving stones with hoses, washing away blood and fish innards into the waters of the canal. Gondoliers transported their customers from shore to shore and shopkeepers loudly rolled up the shutters of their shops. The siesta time was starting.

The detective wanted to take advantage of this odd time, when the city suddenly rested for a few hours, to visit Minutti's widow.

"This man contacted me because he feared for his life. Perhaps he had a particular suspicion. Who else would he confide in if not his wife?"

The boat took us to one of the river palaces near the Rialto Bridge, a water-worn Renaissance structure with a row of arcades, balconies and columns. The boatman stayed at the steps rising straight out of the surface of the water and covered with rotting algae, holding onto the swaying boat, so that we could disembark. Holmes paid him in advance for the return journey to ensure that he would wait for us.

While the man tied the boat to the red and white painted stake, we walked to the doors of the palace, decorated with black grating.

The detective knocked.

A housemaid, a tiny girl with jet-black hair and dark piercing eyes, opened the door. We asked to speak with the lady of the house and were led into the drawing room.

The girl went upstairs to announce our visit, while we made ourselves comfortable in a spacious room decorated with vases and colourful Murano glass accessories. We could distinguish the tiny patter of the housemaid's footsteps above us and heard her knock on the door. The hinges of the door creaked as she entered her employer's room.

Suddenly there was a terrible cry. It cut through the still air of the palace like a scalpel. Apparently the lady of the house was not pleased with our visit.

"*Inglese*! What do they want again? How many times must I tell them? Enough!"

The girl mumbled something.

"Where are they? I will shame them, those hyenas!"

We stood up with astonishment and watched the ceiling swaying under the vigorous footsteps of Signora Minutti.

"We seem to have come at a bad time," said Holmes.

Indeed. The widow of the murdered factory owner literally stormed upon us from the stairs. She was small and thin, dressed in a simple black dress and dark shoes. She wagged her finger in our noses and showered us with insults, which thankfully we did not understand. But she soon switched to English.

"How dare you bother me at this time? And with such a request? My husband would never allow the business to be sold and I shall respect his wishes! It will stay in the family. His death does not change anything!"

We did not have the faintest idea what she was talking about. Then something broke in her, her eyes turned glassy, and she fought back tears.

"I shall not discuss it further. Tell your boss too! Why are you standing here? Go!"

"But we...," said the detective, trying in vain to stop her. She did not give him the opportunity to speak.

"Out! Do not come back!" she cried angrily, pointing a bony finger at the door of the palace.

There was nothing to do. There was no way to reason with such rage and despair. We could only hope to have the opportunity to visit her under more favourable circumstances.

"Signora Teresa, allow me to escort the gentlemen out," said an elegantly dressed man, who had quietly entered the drawing room.

"Please, Luigi, get them out of my sight as quickly as possible," said the widow, turning her back to us.

Her shoulders trembling, Signora Minutti poured herself a glass of water, while the man politely, but unsmilingly, led us out.

Like all Italians he was not particularly big, though his well-tailored coat concealed an athletic figure. His swarthy lightly shaven face shone with manly energy, his dark eyes seemed to notice every detail.

He led us out onto the steps to the canal, where the boatman was waiting. We wanted to board immediately, but the man stopped Holmes.

"Have you gone mad?" he barked at us.

The detective was taken aback and looked at the young man with confusion.

"Pardon me?" he asked coldly, but with renewed interested. "Who are you to talk thus?"

"I am the secretary of the Minutti family, Luigi Pascuale," he said haughtily.

"And this gives you the right to treat us so?"

Pascuale frowned and followed us down the steps to the boat. He took care to ensure that the tips of his expensive well-shined shoes did not touch the water.

"Nobody can hear us here, there is no need to play games," he said angrily. "I clearly told His Lordship to wait! I do not understand why he sent you straight here and just a few days after the funeral. He ought to be aware that it is to no purpose."

Holmes kept a poker face, despite the fact that a moment ago he had no idea why he was being yelled at. But he let Pascuale continue. The people for whom he seemed to have mistaken us for could provide an interesting and illuminating clue.

"Haste will not help us, we need time," said Pascuale. "Come see me tomorrow afternoon at the factory; I will be expecting you at three o'clock. Now go quickly and tell your boss that he does not have to check up on me. I will arrange everything as we agreed. There's no way back anyway."

"No indeed," said Holmes. "We will be there; we wanted to see the factory anyway."

"Of course," Pascuale nodded in a conciliatory manner and even helped us into the boat. It swayed, and as the boatman pushed off the waves lapped hungrily at Pascuale's luxurious shoes.

The secretary cursed and jumped back. He polished the shoe with a handkerchief and disappeared from our view, while we joined the other vessels and drifted away. There was a moment of silence, disturbed only by the sound of the oars hitting the waves.

"Holmes, what just happened?"

"Signora Minutti has apparently mistaken us for an emissary of a British enterprise that is interested in acquiring Minutti's factory. This is important information. Judging by the manner in which she received us she clearly wants to prevent foreigners from taking control of her husband's business. This corresponds with Mycroft's fears."

"What do you make of that awful secretary? What a fop!"

"Mr Pascuale plays a crucial role, Watson! Indeed, he has just admitted that he is working for both sides. He must persuade Mrs Minutti of the necessity of selling."

"Do you think he had a hand in the murder?"

"I cannot say, but I hope we will learn more after our little excursion tomorrow night."

The significance of these words hit me hard.

"We have to figure it out at all costs. If Minutti's factory were to fall into the wrong hands, and should the same appear to be happening to Bollinger, it would be a catastrophe."

"I am aware of that," said Holmes, frowning. He fixed his gaze on the murky waters of the canal.

We drifted onwards between the carefree vessels with their smiling passengers, planning our next steps in the investigation and slowly heading to the one possible solution.

The Island of Death awaited us.

***

The island of San Michele received its grisly moniker at the start of the nineteenth century, when it became the city cemetery.

Although it is located on the Venetian shores, it is separated from the city lagoons by nearly a thousand feet of water. It was briefly used as a jail, but now the island again merely served as a final resting place for the dead.

Behind the high brick wall that surrounded the cemetery we could see the dark green tips of the poplars and the cupolas of the local monastery. The boat, navigated by our local agent Paolo, glided silently across the water to the shores of the island.

Poor Paolo had been dragged here instead of spending a quiet night with his wife and children. As this was hardly an official visit we had had to wait for a dark, moonless night. Personally, I considered it sacrilegious.

"The end justifies the means," Holmes had said back in the hotel. "Or do you perhaps have a better idea?"

Of course I had none.

The detective had opted for a daring and highly illegal course of action. We had no other choice. We desperately needed another clue and the deadly bullet had to be located. Holmes wagered everything on the assumption that the projectile had remained in the victim's body.

"The doctor who performed the autopsy on Minutti did not find the bullet," he said, "but it did not leave the body and therefore must still be inside. It could not have simply vanished into thin air. In my opinion this is a case of bribery or simple negligence. In any event, a crucial clue is missing, and you will help me find it."

"Upon entering the body a bullet sometimes behaves oddly and forgets the laws of physics," I said. "Blood circulation, pressure, deadly cramping of the organs and many other factors could have hidden the bullet from the eyes of the doctor. But must we really break into the cemetery at night, exhume the poor wretch's body and dissect it?"

"We would never obtain official permission here, someone is sabotaging the investigation," he insisted.

He added that he could not embark on the nocturnal mission by himself. My medical knowledge was required in order to determine precisely where the bullet was lodged.

Thus I found myself in the middle of the night at the mooring dock of San Michele, scrambling over the gate of the cemetery in order to desecrate it. Paolo remained at the mooring dock, while Holmes and I silently crept into the cemetery.

The island is divided into several sections, separated from one another by white gravel paths lined with trees. On the far side in front of us loomed the monastery with its Renaissance chapel and urn grove. As Paolo explained to us, there was very little space on the island for graves; therefore the bodies are buried in the ground for only a few years, then are exhumed, cremated and placed in urns.

We headed towards the tombs of eminent figures.

Each of them was a work of art. I would have stopped to take delight in them had not Holmes at that moment removed from the bag a large crowbar and a set of picklocks.

"There's no time to waste, Watson. Please step aside."

He used the picklock to open the padlock hanging on the chain, which held together the wrought iron gate of the Minutti family crypt. The lock gave way with a click and the detective opened the gate. Musty air and dust wafted out.

I placed a handkerchief over my mouth and followed Holmes inside.

We found ourselves surrounded by darkness in a confined space where two adult men could barely stand. The detective lit a torch and examined the tomb. There were marble rectangular sarcophagi, several decades old. In the centre of them stood one that was new and freshly polished.

"The funeral was only a few days ago, the body should not yet be in an advanced state of decay," said Holmes.

My knees wobbled.

The detective swept withered flowers from the sarcophagus and asked me to help him remove the lid. The slab was heavy and my arms were weakened by age and fear. Nevertheless, after much effort and awful creaking we managed to remove it.

Now all that remained was the coffin. Holmes grasped the crowbar and wedged it between the wood of the lid and the sideboard of the casket. The stained oak boards cracked and under the strain of the crowbar the lid came free. We pushed it to the side and stood over the deceased Signor Minutti, dressed for his last journey in a finely tailored Italian suit.

His small body was swollen and the thin pale face was already beginning to lose its features. Alive he clearly was a man who had taken excellent care of himself. The grey hair was cut short and the swollen fingers were adorned with rings.

"Now it is your turn, my friend," said Holmes, unbuttoning the factory owner's shirt.

The first thing I saw was the burned edges of the blackened wound where the bullet had pierced the skin. Stitches from the original autopsy – the one that had not revealed anything – extended across his chest.

I swallowed hard and the detective had to literally push me towards the coffin. My legs refused to budge.

Summoning up every bit of courage, I examined the wound. The skin was still supple, without blood, which had descended and created a purple bedsore on the back of the body.

As though in a dream I cut away Minutti's shirt in order to gain better access to the body. Holmes assisted me and handed me the required instruments. I pulled out the black stitches and re-opened the wound.

The post-mortem under the petroleum light of our torch took almost an hour. I would rather not describe it further: it would be too harrowing for the reader.

I will only say that as soon as I stopped thinking about the circumstances and where I was, my stomach calmed, the nerves and weakness in my legs subsided, and my hands became precise surgical instruments that plunged into the dead body as deftly as they would were he lying on the table in the hospital.

Then I found it!

But at the same moment pandemonium broke loose.

V

The Mysterious Secretary

Everything happened all at once.

My search had just revealed something in Minutti's body that did not belong there: a strange metal fragment. But before Holmes and I could examine it more closely, we heard the excited shouting of night watchmen. They must have discovered that someone else was on the island. If they found us it would be hard to explain what we were up to.

"They are searching the island," said the detective calmly, peaking out of the tomb. "Three watchmen with lamps; it will take them about ten minutes to reach us. They have not discovered Paolo yet, but he must have heard them. If he has any sense of self-preservation he has no doubt rowed away and I would not rely on his returning for us."

"He left without us?" I asked, terrified. "What will we do?"

"Swim," he said. "We must get out of here as quickly as possible."

"But we cannot just leave him here like this," I said pointing to Minutti's open grave.

Nor was I ready to leave; my coat and medical instruments were lying everywhere.

"Very well then; we have four minutes before we need to depart, so let us make haste," said Holmes.

I carefully cleaned the metal fragment that I had found in Minutti's body, wrapped it in a handkerchief and put it in my pocket. Then I stitched the industrialist's chest back together. The detective meanwhile rapidly cleaned the tomb, gathered up all the instruments into the bag, and when we were both ready he helped me arrange Minutti's clothes and return the body to the dignified position in which we had found it.

Then we quietly shut the coffin and the lid of the sarcophagus. To this day I still do not understand how I managed do to it without it falling from my trembling fingers and loudly breaking. We extinguished the lamp, lucky that as yet nobody had seen us. I pressed the medical bag to my chest and felt my heart racing.

"The lights are nearing, it's now or never!" said Holmes.

We stole out of the tomb, the detective closing the gate behind us, and ran out among the shadows to the wall. We caught our breath for a moment and continued along the wall to the gate of the island cemetery. The watchmen passed us through the archway and headed in staggered formation to the centre of the cemetery.

When they had vanished from our sight we clambered back over the gate and scurried to the dock, where to our dismay we discovered that Holmes had surmised correctly. Paolo and the boat were gone.

Unfortunately there was no other boat that we could take for the journey back.

The voices coming from the cemetery grew louder and more excited, which surely meant that the watchmen had discovered the open tomb, though we had left everything in order inside. Fortunately it did not occur to them to search each coffin and they apparently concluded that the robbers had escaped. At least I prayed this was the case.

But praying was not enough for Holmes.

"Take off your jacket, shoes and trousers," he said, doing likewise.

He hid the medical bag and the lamp in a bush by the wall, tied our clothes in a bundle and plunged into the water.

I felt like crying. Unless I wanted to lose my good reputation and trade my career as a doctor for that of a convicted grave robber I had to follow him. I sat down on the wharf and slid slowly into the water.

The sea reeked and despite the warm spring weather was so cold as to make our teeth chatter. The detective set the tempo and holding our clothes above the surface of the water, we swam away from the island in the direction of the glowing city.

I could tell from the way he breathed that this was no easy task for him.

"I recall how you used to urge me to take more exercise," he said when we had a chance to rest for a moment.

We treaded water side by side and tried not to notice the dead pigeon that bobbed nearby.

"Really?"

"As I now feel another coronary coming on it was no doubt sound advice," he smiled.

I was grateful to him for attempting to cheer me up.

Suddenly we heard a splash in the dark, like waves lapping against the hull of a boat.

We lowered our voices for fear that we were being followed, but from the dark emerged the silhouette of our dear friend Paolo. We could not have been happier to see anyone at that moment. He shone a lamp on us and helped us out of the water. I was the first to scramble aboard and Holmes passed me the bundle of clothes which he had protected from the water.

Thanks to this effort we were able to shed our wet shirts and put on dry ones.

"You were very fortunate," said Paolo.

He told us that the clamour had started when the gatekeeper had been awoken by the noise of a cat stepping on a branch. Paolo explained apologetically that he had been unable to warn us, because it would have led to his discovery, which would have been of no help to us.

We waited in his boat for a few more minutes until the confusion on the island subsided and the light of the watchmen searching the harbour disappeared, and returned for our things. They were still hidden in the bush where Holmes had left them.

Paolo then took us via the Grand Canal to our hotel. Tired and cold we finally climbed into our beds just before dawn. In my pocket, however, was the metal fragment, which would no doubt provide many answers.

***

Holmes was the first to rise. His mind could not rest when it swarmed with so many questions. Nor did he let me sleep. I woke up after a mere four hours of rest and dragged myself to the dining room for breakfast. Holmes was devouring his food. My stomach, on the other hand, was still turning after the night's adventures and I was unable to swallow more than a cup of tea.

Upon returning to the room I too resembled a dead body.

"Pull yourself together, Watson," Holmes admonished. "We will have plenty of time to rest later. Now we must work for the future of our country!"

"I am no doubt suffering from a lack of adrenaline, which fuels the brain."

"Indeed, and yesterday it seemed that we gave you a little too much."

"Please do not remind me," I said, preferring to concentrate on the facts that the detective requested.

I pondered, returning in my mind to Minutti's tomb, and began itemising the details.

"During the autopsy, short as it was, I arrived at a number of significant facts. You were right in calling it indispensable."

The detective bid me describe what I had in mind.

"As far as I know, in the official materials from Paolo the autopsy was described too briefly. It was limited to the conclusion that the bullet was not discovered in the victim's body, and thus the matter was closed."

"Precisely."

"That is why I was surprised by what I found when I opened the body. Some of the organs − the heart, lungs, stomach, intestines − were badly torn, which is what caused Minutti's death. I am surprised that the court doctor did not mention this."

"It does not surprise me at all," said Holmes, shrugging. "We continue to uncover facts that suggest someone has been thwarting the investigation. Could this damage to the organs have been caused in the course of the autopsy?"

"No doctor, regardless of whether he had been bribed, would treat a dead body this way."

"How could one bullet cause the injuries that you describe?" the detective asked. "According to the initial examination he was shot only once."

"It could not," I replied. "Certainly no ordinary bullet."

"What do you mean?"

"The way in which the organs were perforated is very specific. I have seen it before, during my military service.[15] It is as though something exploded inside him. The internal damage corresponds to that caused by shrapnel from an explosive."

I of course realised how absurd it sounded.

"Minutti could not have been killed by a grenade, his body would be in another state entirely!" said Holmes, pacing. "Are you certain?"

"Completely. Anyone who has seen internal organs ripped apart by a grenade never forgets."

"Forgive me, my friend; I did not mean to doubt your conclusions. It is quite far-fetched. But it does explain the absence of a bullet and the fragment."

"As a doctor I can suggest one explanation," I said. "The bullet entered the body, shattered inside, exploded and its shards caused the destructive whirlwind. Of course it then could not be found in the body, for it no longer existed. And nobody noticed those tiny shards, as they were not looking for them."

---

[15] We know that Watson's military career was less than brilliant. Upon gaining his medical degree he studied to be a military doctor and in 1879 he enlisted in this capacity with the Fifth Royal Northumberland Fusiliers in India. After transferring to the Berkshire regiment during the Second Anglo-Afghan War, however, he was wounded in action at the Battle of Maiwand on 28 July 1880. Recovering from severe intestinal disease he returned to England and in early January 1881 met Sherlock Holmes.

Holmes stopped pacing the room and looked at me with surprise.

"Watson, it seems that you have hit the nail on the head!" he cried, his face brightening.

I was glad that I could help him and that for once I did not have to play the role of baffled simpleton.

I settled contentedly into an armchair and savoured the feeling.

"You are definitely right," said Holmes, developing my theory further. "That would mean, of course, that Minutti was shot with a hitherto unknown type of firearm. I have never in my life heard of the type of shrapnel projectile that you describe."

Neither had I. But the detective certainly had a fair notion of who would know more about such advancements in weaponry.

It thus had come time to fulfil a promise.

***

Minutti's factories were spread throughout northern Italy, but the most important one, the arms factory, was near Venice. We headed there at the invitation of Luigi Pascuale, the family secretary, who had behaved so suspiciously when we visited Minutti's widow.

In the afternoon we boarded the train, crossed the bridge connecting Venice with the mainland, and headed to the industrial heart of the city. The journey took us about an hour, during which the detective advanced several of his theories. So far he had only tentatively connected bits of information and was attempting to find a connection between them. But there were so many unknowns that it was merely a mental exercise rather than a real attempt to solve the case.

Soon we arrived in Valeri, a sleepy provincial town whose only attraction was the Minutti Fabbrica Di Armi. We announced ourselves to the guard at the gatehouse in the clay courtyard adjoining the factory. It consisted of the two brick wings of the production hall with a smokestack, warehouse and administrative building. Operations were in full swing; some one hundred workers were labouring and the gates of the factory presently opened to let out a lorry fully loaded with sealed crates.

We waited for a long time outside; perhaps so that Mr Pascuale could make it clear to us that we were not worth hurrying for, despite the fact that we represented someone of importance.

Pascuale's assistant, a dour blonde with a rather masculine manner, whose stern expression and dull clothes did not at all correspond to her age, then led us to the highest floor of the administrative building where the secretary's office neighboured the now empty office of Vito Minutti. Both could be entered from the hallway and the anteroom where the assistant had her desk.

"Gentlemen, welcome to the factory," said Pascuale from behind his desk as soon as we entered. "Please pardon the delay, but after this tragic event we naturally had to increase security measures."

He bade us sit down on a large leather sofa and ordered the assistant to bring refreshments. He waited for the woman to finish serving us and as soon as she left his expression changed.

67

He stood up, took off his jacket, threw it over the backrest of his chair and rolled up the sleeves of his silk shirt. I thought for a moment that he wanted to give us a thrashing, but he only sat down close to us, drank slowly and crossed one leg over the other.

"Your visit surprised me," he said, trying to confuse us with his superior manner, which only hid his nervousness. "We agreed that you would leave everything to me."

Remaining silent at the right moment can be much more effective than asking questions, so we did not react.

"Was it a good decision?" asked Holmes.

As expected, this released an avalanche.

"Does his Lordship doubt me?" cried Pascuale, practically jumping off of the sofa. "He himself was clearly convinced that it is impossible to negotiate with the Minuttis! It did not work with the old man and it will not with Signora Teresa. His death – which I don't want to know anything about – did not help you at all in this regard. Your visit yesterday only angered the Signora and strengthened her resolve. If you do not convince her to sell, I am your only key to the factory!"

"We just want to ensure that they key does not get jammed in the lock."

"You need not worry about that. I am aware of how deep I have gone, as you must surely realise. In the meantime I will run the company according to the instructions as promised. The family trusts me completely; Sir Rupert can be certain of that."

We had caught the name, thrown into the air with the utmost carelessness. I noticed how Holmes's ears pricked up. The young *consigliere*, however, probably for security reasons and according to instructions, did not utter his future employer's surname.

"All right," said the detective. "All must continue as was agreed."

His relief was evident.

"Gentlemen, I did not mean to be rude to you. After all, the three of us get our orders from the same boss. I just lost my nerve when I saw you in the palace. The lady is very excitable; it is always a struggle for me to get her to make the right decisions and any pressure could destroy my work."

"After Minutti's death you became the helmsman of his empire."

"I could not put it better myself," said Pascuale. "Do you have a cheque for me?"

Holmes was taken aback.

"No," he said, shaking his head slowly. "But you will receive it shortly."

"In the regular way?"

"Of course," said the detective. "And lest I forget, Sir Rupert also asked us to personally assure him that your plans regarding the secret investigation are safe and that nobody else can obtain them."

"You can assure him that they are in my safekeeping."

"May we see them?"

Pascuale was taken aback momentarily, but then reluctantly stood up, returned to his desk and removed a key. He walked to the wall, which contained a steel safe, unlocked it, entered the combination and swung open the heavy door. From where we were seated we could see that the safe was divided into compartments full of documents. There was also money, laid out in neat stacks, and a cloth tube. Luigi removed it and brought it over to us.

"Gentlemen, please convince yourselves that everything is in order," he said, opening the tube and pulling out a roll of blueprints. "These are the specifications for a tracked vehicle for rugged terrain, samples for deadly chemical substances and explosive bullets for our special guns."

The detective quickly surveyed the plans. I knew that he was trying to remember as many details as possible.

"Does Sir Rupert also have all of these plans?"

"Of course, I sent them to him several months ago," Pascuale confirmed.

"Then everything is in order," said Holmes, returning the roll to him. "Guard it carefully. This could mean a revolution in the arms industry, and if worse came to worst, it will help us win the war!"

"Those were Sir Rupert's words exactly," said Pascuale, rolling up the plans and returning them to the tube.

He sealed it and locked it back in the impregnable safe.

It occurred to me to ask whether there was a prototype of these things, in particular as the kind of gun that we had seen on the paper corresponded to what may have killed Minutti.

My impetuous question almost gave us away. The secretary's eyes
narrowed with suspicion.

"No," he replied deliberately. "Signor Minutti refused to make these weapons as he considered them too barbarous. He did not even want to hear of them. But you must have known that, no?"

I froze, not knowing what to say. But the detective saved the situation.

"You did not understand the question, sir," said Holmes calmly. "My colleague was simply wondering whether you personally have initiated steps towards their production."

Pascuale took offence and immediately forgot his suspicions.

"I received no instruction. I assumed that his Lordship would take care of this in one of his other factories!"

"Very well," said Holmes, rising. "There is no reason for concern. Continue working according to the original instructions, as though we were not here."

"If this was meant to be a surprise inspection I am happy that I have stood the test."

"You said it yourself," said the detective, slapping him on the shoulder. We then bade him a hasty goodbye, saying that we were in a hurry to catch a train.

The assistant escorted us out and we headed to Valeri station in order to make the connection to Venice.

We settled on a bench on the platform, basking in the pleasant sunshine. Holmes for the second time that day attempted to piece together the various clues. After our visit to the factory many things had become clearer.

"I now know without a shadow of doubt that a certain Sir Rupert is behind Minutti's death," he said. "The given name corresponds to that of the man who issued the cheque for my death to Pastor Barlow. A concrete motive is also starting to form. Mycroft was right to fear the changing influence in the leadership of important European arms factories. His Lordship

71

perhaps was not able to buy Minutti's factory, but with secretary Pascuale in place and the police bought off, he does not need to. And he already has obtained their patents."

"But Pascuale himself did not murder him."

"No he did not," agreed the detective. "Mr Pascuale may be capable of selling his own grandmother, but I do not believe he would kill his master in cold blood. Besides, he has a watertight alibi. He was abroad at the time of Minutti's murder."

"Perhaps now with the help of your brother we will succeed in determining the full name of this scoundrel. And then we can put the screws on Pastor Barlow!"

"Watson, where does this lust for revenge come from?" laughed Holmes. "Nevertheless, you are right; there is no longer a reason to protect him. As soon as we return to England we will pay him a visit. We must also find out who inherits the companies in the case of Lord Bollinger's death and find this person's connection to Sir Rupert. This will be the key to solving the case."

"Do you think Bollinger is dead?"

"I hope not, but we must be prepared for the worst."

"What about those weapons?"

"The explosive bullet assembled according to the secret plans of Minutti himself was designed to confuse investigators and act as an insurance policy if the bribes failed. But we still do not know who pulled the trigger. Our mysterious nobleman certainly did not sully his hands. Nevertheless, the circle of suspects has been narrowed."

"But what is the reason?" I asked. "So far it does not appear to be political."

"At this point nothing occurs to me besides industrial espionage, and of course money, the oldest motive in the world," said Holmes. "In this day and age, when we are all engaged in war, whoever controls the arms industry has the power to dictate terms."

"War: even the word itself clouds men's minds," I sighed.

The detective said something else, but his words were lost in the whistling of the arriving locomotive.

We returned to Venice and to our hotel. On the way we stopped at the drop off point to pick up a message from Paolo and leave him a reply.

One that would cost the poor fellow his life.

VI
Death on the Canal

The message from Paolo contained good and bad news. In it Mycroft told us that he had succeeded in obtaining a list of Silver Ghost owners, and wrote us the only name that corresponded with the letters in the signature which Holmes had deciphered. Rupert H. Darringford. *Touché*! We were one step closer. The secret service was already verifying it and promised quick results as long as it was not an alias. The other group, on the hunt for Lord Bollinger independently from us, so far had not reported any success.

The second part of the letter did not cheer us. It revealed that we would not have the good fortune to interrogate Barlow. It seemed that the earth had swallowed up the wheezing churchman, who had disappeared with surprising speed and with all the money that he had managed to withdraw from the bank. Nor had he neglected to sweep up his tracks at the parish. According to Mycroft's agents, this occurred soon after our departure from Fulworth and before the arrival of the men charged with tracking down the pastor.

"As soon as we succeed in opening one door, another one closes in the draft," Holmes complained. "Nevertheless, we must persist, my friend, we must persist!"

He hurriedly scrawled a few sentences for Paolo in reply and while I covered him he hid the paper in a chink in the cover of the cast-iron candelabra lamp. Then we went to the hotel.

It happened soon after night fell over the city and the Venetian palaces became enshrouded in a golden robe of artificial light. A terrified scream echoed over the canal. It broke through the embankment all the way to our window and alarmed all the local residents in the block.

In the houses along the water the wooden shutters opened all at once, as though the old palaces were opening their tired eyes. The detective and I also looked out. The piteous howling of a woman, standing in the street in the middle of her spilled shopping, led our gaze to the canal.

Lying face down in the water was the body of a dead man. As always, whenever death appeared nearby, it piqued Holmes's interest.

"Let us go take a look," he said to me, putting on his overcoat.

We ran downstairs and arrived at the body before the police.

A gondolier had pulled the body up onto the shore and examined it to see if there was any point in attempting to revive him. But it was hopeless, as I could see at first glance. According to the colour of the skin the body had been in the water for too long.

But my initial professional interest suddenly turned to horror when I saw the face of the dead man. The detective also recognised him at the same time.

Lying at our feet on the embankment was Paolo.

"My God," I cried.

I pushed aside the gondolier and kneeled next to the body. I moved the wet hair from the face and slapped it on the cheeks in a foolish attempt to revive the body. He had foam in his mouth and the water on his face smelled of grease.

I looked desperately at Holmes.

"We cannot help him," he mumbled and knelt down next to us.

He closed the poor wretch's eyelids and looked through his pockets. He frisked the soaked jacket and the pockets of the lining. None of the observers had the courage to protest.

"Are you looking for something?"

"His wallet. Aha, here it is!" said the detective, opening the leather portmanteau.

I winced when he removed a photograph of Paolo's wife and children. There was also some money, from which Holmes deduced that the motive had not been robbery. Even his watch was still there. Otherwise the pockets of the jacket, vest and trousers were empty.

A *carabinier* finally appeared in the crowd.

The detective returned the wallet to the pocket and quickly surveyed the body before the police sealed off the area. There was nothing more that we could do besides stand silently by during the official examination.

"We ought to get out of here," Holmes whispered to me. "I would not want someone to take notice of us and potentially take us in for questioning. It might reveal our connection to Paolo."

It was easy to disappear, as the crowd kept pushing forward, and hence squeezed us out.

Holmes took me aside in order to collect his thoughts. He left me in front of the hotel and ran across the bridge to the illuminated island under the lamp on the other side of the canal in order to check the drop off point.

"Just as I feared," he said when he returned.

In my heart I was still with dear Paolo and his family, so I had to ask him to explain what he meant. I was not capable of reflection.

"The drop off point is empty," said the detective. "Somebody must have followed us, seen how we placed the message inside and waited for Paolo to come pick it up."

"Followed us?" I cried.

"Yes, just as Paolo feared at our first meeting. Fool that I am, I thought his fears unfounded. I was quite wrong!"

"How awful!"

A police boat neared upon the water. The officers hopped out onto the bank and started to ask questions among the bystanders. They were looking for the woman who had discovered the body, and soon they naturally also learned about the two unknown men who had taken an interest in the body.

But we were already safe. Holmes's thoughts were still occupied with Paolo's murder.

"He drowned," said the detective later that night when we returned to the hotel. "This was preceded by a struggle, probably following a sudden ambush."

"On what do you base your assumptions?"

"I discovered a wound on the back of his head. It was not large enough to have been the primary cause of death; the attack from behind only stunned him. It clearly was not planned; this can be seen in the murder weapon, which was no doubt a randomly picked up stone. Then the murderer pushed him in the water and made sure that he was not swimming."

"How brutal!"

"The angle of the hit and the power with which it was struck also suggest to me another interesting fact. This was a smaller person, not possessing great strength. I might almost say that it was a woman."

"What woman would be capable of such a cold-hearted and premeditated murder?" I said, struggling to believe it.

"I haven't the slightest idea, Watson. Please give me a moment to think; I must have peace and quiet."

With these words he fell into a long silence, from which I did not want to disturb him further. I left him on the terrace of our hotel while I sampled a cigar and a bottle of the light local wine. Then I went to bed.

Just as I expected, however, this night too would be neither peaceful nor quiet.

After a few hours of sleep I felt somebody shaking me by the shoulder. It was Holmes. Clearly he had not gone to sleep at all. His eyes were bloodshot and there were deep circles beneath them. Evidently he had been thinking about the case the whole time.

"Get up," he said. "We must go!"

"Have you gone mad? At this hour?" I said, drawing the blanket over my head. "It is still dark out! What would we do?"

"It will be daybreak soon," he continued. "And Paolo's murderer already has a big head start. I would not like to give him even more time to escape."

Sighing, I yielded and pulled on my trousers and jacket. While the city slept we stole out of the hotel and returned to the spot where the dead body had been discovered.

All was peaceful. Nothing attested to the tragedy that had taken place here only a few hours earlier. The police had taken away the body, the crowd had left long ago, and the rats and pigeons had taken care of the bread that the terrified woman had spilled.

"What are we looking for? The corpse was carried here by the water and all of the tracks have floated away."

"You must not give up so easily," said the detective. "How many times have we faced a case that seemed unsolvable only to succeed in cracking it?"

Although he was undoubtedly correct, I was curious to see what the detective would do next. To my surprise he lay down on his stomach, leaned over the curb of the embankment, and put his hand in the water.

"Paolo's body was discovered after nine o'clock in the evening," said Holmes. "We left him the message at five. As he picked it up, it is clear that he died some time in between. The body was unusually cold; it had been lying in the water for more than an hour, which narrows the time of death even more. I believe that it happened at dusk, when the shadows lengthen."

He was no doubt correct. Even I was capable of making these deductions. But I still did not understand how the time of death would help us uncover the identity of the murderer.

But the detective was far from finished.

"The water is rather warm," he said, swishing his fingers in the canal. "Its corridor is wide and most of the day the sun shines on it."

"My theory," he continued, drying his fingers on his coat, "is that the body floated here from one of the tributaries, which are narrow and shady. And those winding streets around them practically invite wrongdoing."

I glanced around both sides of the canal, which was one of the main city communications, and which after several hundred yards flowed into the Grand Canal.

"But there are dozens of these side streams!"

"Use your brain, my friend! I know that I pulled you out of bed at an ungodly hour, but even in this condition you are capable of deducing this basic physical fact!"

"Currents!" I cried. "All we have to do is figure out where they go and they will lead us to the site of the murder!"

"You see, you are not so poorly off after all," said the detective, slapping me on the shoulder. "But that is not all. At such a busy hour Paolo would not float along the surface more than a few minutes without being discovered. I think we ought to head to the closest stream against the current, which is this one."

He was pointing at a rivulet on the other side of the canal. We crossed the arched bridge and headed towards it.

It was a typical Venetian rivulet, just a few yards wide, hardly big enough for a craft to pass through, and with a humble walkway running alongside it. On both sides rose the flaking walls of a palace, above which shone the first rays of the morning sun.

For the first time I felt just how confined the city really was. We could not even walk side by side and we had to proceed in single file. Venice suddenly began to feel rotten, as though something distasteful and corrupted were lurking behind the romantic facade and glistening surface of the Grand Canal.

After a few hundred yards the rivulet forked, merging into two other canals, along which the walkway was even narrower. Laundry hung on lines between the houses: shirts, stockings, trousers and striped gondoliers´ leotards. Above the water rose a strange haze; everything suggested that visitors were unwelcome.

"Where to now?"

"Each of us will take one side. If either of us comes across anything suspicious we will signal the other."

Without waiting for me to reply he plunged into the morning gloom of the street on his right.

I never would have told him that I was afraid, but I humbly admit to you, dear reader, that I was terrified. As his footsteps grew more distant a shiver went down my spine. I was alone against a narrow and twisting wall, the air smelled of sewerage, and just a few hours earlier our friend had lost his life somewhere here. I would not be surprised were some rogue to take mine as well. I could only hope that the criminals were still fast asleep in their beds.

I started off on the opposite side from where Holmes had disappeared and carefully stepped along the cobblestones. Behind the closed windows above me Venice started to awaken. Coffee was brewing, kettles were whistling, toilets were flushing.

All of these sounds terrified me and distracted me from what the detective had asked me to do. If a letter from the murderer with an exact description of how he had killed Paolo were lying in plain view, I surely would not have noticed it.

I had already gone quite a ways from the crossroads where we had separated when from a distance I heard Holmes calling.

Exhaling with the relief of not having to continue along the dark and unfriendly street, I ran back. A few yards after the confluence of the canal I found the detective kneeling at the edge of the bank and staring at the water.

"What did you find?"

"A stain," he said.

Indeed, on the surface of the water together with other waste floated an odd greasy stain. It was slowly dissolving in the water, but more grease flowed from the ducts protruding into the canal from grooves in the pavement. Perhaps it came from the drainage of one of the restaurants.

"You surely must have noticed that Paolo's clothes were greasy. It is likely that the water carried him from here."

I looked in the direction in which he pointed. Nearby the current flowed into another, wider canal.

"Our friend drowned somewhere between this spot and the start of the street. If we thoroughly search the pavement and the banks we will no doubt find clues."

Like a bloodhound that has found the trail, the detective began scanning the ground yard by yard. The morning light was gaining in intensity and it was only a matter of ten or twenty minutes before people would begin to appear and the water would be filled with rowboats and gondolas.

I also searched, though I did not know precisely for what. Holmes fortunately was not counting on me.

"Eureka!" he cried presently, picking up from the ground a cobblestone lying haphazardly in a puddle under a gutter. "If I am not mistaken this is the murder weapon! The edge of the stone corresponds to the size of the wound in Paolo's skull and confirms my theory that the killer used the first thing he could find."

Upon closer examination of the stone we found dark and smudgy stains resembling human blood.

"You see, it is not difficult to calculate the exact time of death when we measure the speed of the current of all the canals through which the body floated and consider the distance which it travelled. I do not think that it will differ much from my estimate."

"We now know where and how the murder occurred," I said, "but I still do not understand how it will get us closer to the murderer. The water washed off the fingerprints and it is hardly likely we will find any witnesses."

"The time has come for real detective work!" said Holmes, removing from his pocket his indispensable magnifying glass. He bent over the pavement and despite his rheumatism paced quickly back and forth with his nose just an inch from the surface.

The bulldog persistence with which he had apprehended so many criminals was again in evidence.

"You see how the mildew on the curb is scraped off here, whereas elsewhere there is an unbroken mossy growth?" he pointed out. "This is where the killer dragged the unconscious Paolo to the water and threw him in."

The detective knelt on the damp cobblestones and examined the spot more closely. A short distance from us the doors of a house opened and a worker emerged. Unfortunately he was headed towards the spot that my companion was currently examining.

"Make certain nobody walks here!" Holmes barked. "I only need a few more minutes!"

I stopped the sleepy man and asked him to take a different route, hoping against hope that no one else would come. I did not want to get into a skirmish with a gondolier's fists.

Another whoop from the detective allayed my fears. He put away the magnifying glass and between the place where we found the rock and where Paolo's body had been thrown into the water he used his pocket knife to pick up a cobblestone and proudly showed me the soil sticking to it.

"This soil is the answer to our entire investigation," he explained to me, as clearly I was unable to follow the trail of his logical deductions. "You will not find this soil in all of Venice. The local soil is coarse and dark with a large proportion of sand. But the soil that I am holding in my hand was brought here on the shoes of the murderer, probably a size five."

"I assume you already know where the soil comes from," I said.

"Reddish clay mixed with brick dust is quite uncommon. But we were walking on it yesterday in the courtyard of the Minutti factory."

"They followed us from there!"

"He followed us," Holmes corrected me. "There was only one killer."

"How can you be certain?"

"The clues and simple logic, my friend. The spontaneous nature of the murder, confirmed by the murder weapon that we found, testifies to the fact that it was not planned. Somebody from the factory was suspicious about us and followed us. And he needed to know who would collect our message."

"But there was not much in it."

"No, but it makes clear that we are not who we pretended to be in the factory. And although at first he only shadowed Paolo, he then decided to kill him. He pushed him into the water and perhaps even waited to make certain that he would not swim out alive."

"We must assume that Lord Darringford already knows about our investigation."

"Yes, Paolo's death has deprived us of an important ally and a pair of trump cards."

"And who is the murderer?"

"Isn't it obvious!" said the detective, waving his hands. "Think, Watson: A woman, I'd say about five foot seven, who could have followed us from the factory. She is not too strong, but has the guile and resolve to murder a stronger man."

"That Amazon! Pascuale's secretary!"

"Yes. A woman who moves about in the man's world and intends to make her mark in it."

I shook my head incredulously. Another persistent thought sprang to my mind.

"I know what you're thinking," Holmes interjected, as though reading my thoughts. "It occurred to me too that Paolo was not her first victim. If she indeed killed Minutti, however, it means that she is Lord Darringford's right hand in the factory, no matter what Signor Pascuale thinks."

"The corrupt *consigliere* overestimated his importance."

"Naturally he too served a purpose. Betrayal. He sold Minutti's patents while the factory owner was still alive. Darringford thus stole the prototype weapon in cold blood."

"What next?" I asked as we made our way back to the hotel.

"I think there is nothing else for us in Venice," the detective replied. "I do not think that we will see that woman here again. She has done what she needed to do; she knows that we will come after her, and we do not have any evidence against Pascuale. Do not forget that we are here in secret; we cannot go to the police."

My friend was right.

We spent another two days in Italy, but found no clues that would lead us to Paolo's murderer. She had vanished. Whoever Lord Darringford was, he knew how to erase all traces of his people.

It was time for us to return to England.

But there was still one more surprise for us in Italy before our departure. Upon returning to the hotel from our last walk through the streets and bridges of Venice we found an eerie message. Nailed to the door of our room was a golden carnival mask, its androgynous features twisted in a malicious smile.

VII
A Duet for Violin and Violoncello

Nothing much had changed in London during our weeklong absence. The newspapers grinded out the same stories; Mycroft moved between his apartment in the Pall Mall, the Diogenes Club and his office in Westminster; and the King[16] was increasingly anxious about the disappearance of Albert Bollinger.

My wife, who apparently assumed that I would be away longer, had left town to visit her relatives. I put Holmes up in our guest room and the next afternoon Mycroft came over and the three of us planned what to do next over a bottle of red wine.

We related everything that had happened in Italy, including our meeting with Luigi Pascuale, who had taken over the management of Minutti's factory. Mycroft informed us that if Bollinger were declared dead, the nobleman's sister Emily would inherit the family business.

"I doubt she would allow the business to be managed by a secretary or anyone she does not know," said Mycroft. "She is a very determined and resourceful lady who likes to keep a firm grasp on things. We must seek another motive for Bollinger's kidnapping besides a desire to take over his business."

He also had news for us concerning Rupert Darringford. The son of a noble country family, he was a rich man with an unremarkable past. We even obtained his photograph, in which we clearly recognised the man who had stormed out of Pastor

---

[16] George V, the first monarch of the House of Windsor, who reigned from 1910 to 1926.

Barlow's house. The pieces of the puzzle were finally falling into place.

"Darringford, the family estate in Scotland, is looked after by servants. Lord Rupert is the last living male heir to the title. He was never very popular in society, unlike his sister. They say that he suffers from a kind of mental disorder. But it may just be slander. For the time being, however, we cannot arrest him. We lack evidence, as he has been living in seclusion for several years; and he constantly travels, although nobody knows his present whereabouts."

"I certainly wonder what he is up to," said Holmes. "Why would he want to control Minutti's business? Money? By all accounts he is already vastly wealthy. Patent theft? Espionage? But to whose benefit? Was he responsible for the attack on me? In all probability, yes. He will not hesitate to kill further and will stop at nothing."

"His sister Alice Darringford lives near London, you ought to start with her," said Mycroft, handing his brother a dossier. "Here is the information that we managed to obtain. There is also a dossier about Bollinger. We are beginning to lose hope that he is still alive."

"I had hoped that in Venice we would uncover the connection between his disappearance and Minutti's death," said the detective sadly.

"Nobody sees it as a failure," said his brother. "The case is intricate and our theories are hazy at best."

"We ought to have been more careful," said Holmes. "Perhaps I am too old and have been too long in retirement. I acted rashly, like a bull in a china shop."

"Nonsense!" I cried.

"I agree with the doctor, Sherlock. Put such thoughts out of your mind; I need you to be as charming as possible tomorrow evening."

Holmes looked at his brother with suspicion.

"You know that I hate parties."

"Ah, but you will go to this one, it is work related," said Mycroft, taking from his pocket an invitation to the garden party in the luxurious villa of Lady Darringford. "It is an event for the nobility, so do try to play the part. There will be no better opportunity to get close to Lady Darringford and to obtain as much information about her brother as possible."

The detective did not know whether to rejoice or despair. Naturally we could not have hoped for anything better. He graciously took the invitation and read it. It was for Mr Cedric Parker and Dr John Watson.

Sighing he placed it on the table and for the rest of the day made himself scarce.

***

He only emerged from his shell in the evening before the event. Perhaps he was conserving his energy to help him endure the party, but at the strike of six he stood in the vestibule dressed in his best tailcoat, which he had had Mrs Hudson send over from the farm.

"I have not worn it in several years, but it still fits, wouldn't you say?"

Indeed it did.

Holmes's physique was just as lithe and slim as ever, hence the suit fit as though it had been made to measure the day before. Mrs Hudson looked after his things with great care. The tailcoat and trousers were carefully brushed and ironed, and kept free of moths. He matched the suit with a starched white shirt and collar and black bowtie. As always he radiated dignity and nobility.

I too was ready. I opted for a classically cut summer suit with a necktie. We were ready to depart. The carriage was waiting.

We arrived at Alice Darringford's villa, or rather palace, shortly before seven o'clock. Guests from far and wide were already arriving. A long line of automobiles, *fiacres* and carriages streamed in along the road from London, passing through the main gates at less than one minute intervals. There were so many of them that the coachmen and chauffeurs had to jostle and compete for who would unload their passengers first. We disembarked onto the vast marble steps lit by torches and leading to the widely opened doors of the opulent mansion.

Holmes proceeded up the steps as though he were dragging an iron ball on his leg.

I had to laugh.

At the entrance a footman in livery sidled up to us and offered us champagne. We drank it and plunged into the crowd. The vestibule already contained many notables. I recognised several politicians and actors, and there were also industrialists and members of noble families. Their wives wore the most opulent jewels, which danced in the light of the crystal chandelier above our heads. From both sides of the hall a staircase rose to the upper floor of the house; on the right was an immense drawing room and French doors leading to the garden.

The guests conversed in a lively manner while a six-piece orchestra played gently in the background.

We walked through the villa, politely conversing with people whom I knew mainly by reputation in a manner that Holmes derisively called "a variant of empty chatter". Personally I was fascinated by how some people could carry on a ten-minute monologue without actually saying anything.

Two hours passed in this way without us even seeing our hostess. Finally we walked out into the garden. The sky had already darkened and silver stars shone down on the illuminated garden.

À propos of that garden! The architect must have lavished it with attention. The lawns, shrubs, trees, beds of exotic flowers, everything was designed in charming and brilliant combinations of colours and shapes, and it was all perfectly maintained. It was especially magnificent now in the spring. I guessed that one of the reasons for the festivities was the proud owner's desire to show off her hobby.

"Lady Darringford certainly has taste and a weakness for fine things," said Holmes. "I feel as though I am in Versailles."

We set off on a short tour of the park, further from the merry company and the light of the lamps, in order to rest from the noise of the party, which was already making my head spin, and take some fresh air. We made it all the way to a beech grove next to an old gazebo.

The mighty crowns of the trees had a regular egg-shaped form and the trunks were textbook slim, covered in a thin light-grey bark with a slight blue tinge. On the ground lay achenes and near them were freshly planted rhododendrons.

"The architect did not succeed in this part of the garden," said Holmes. He was referring to the lack of taste reflected in the gazebo, which was begging to be torn down, and the disparate combination of trees. Nevertheless the shrubs smelled beautifully and had a calming effect. We were ready to head back to the whirlwind of society in the centre of the garden.

"Watson, is that you?" we suddenly heard in the dark. "I can't believe it!"

The lawn was overflowing with people, so at first I did not know who was calling. From a cluster of guests emerged a tall man in a red officer's uniform, waving at me in a friendly manner.

I only recognised him when he came closer and his face with its rust-coloured sideburns shone in the light of one of the lamps. It was Pankhurst, my old friend from my student years.

"How long has it been since I've seen you!" he boomed. "Hell, at least thirty, forty years![17] But don't think I've lost track of you. I literally devour your stories about that famous detective. They are simply exceptional!"

"Thank you, Pankhurst, I am happy to see you again too," I said, shaking his hand.

"Is it true what I have heard? That Holmes is dead?"

"Sadly, yes. This is Mr Parker, Holmes's cousin," I said, introducing the detective, who had been standing silently a short distance away.

The officer took off his hat and shook both of our hands.

"My condolences to both of you. England has lost a great man. He embodied the values that we all believe in."

---

[17] The acquaintance probably dates back to the early 1870s when Watson started studying medicine at the University of London.

"And what are you doing here, old friend?" I said, steering the conversation elsewhere, despite the fact that Holmes looked as though listening to someone singing his praises interested him.

"Well," said the old soldier waving his hand and barely able to contain a disgusted grimace. "I am here because of my youngest daughter, Grace. I am her escort. You see, my friend, I can tell you: she is unmarried and I fear that she will remain so for a long time. Not that she isn't pretty, mind you. But she has taken up these modern feminist ideas and considers men as just a necessary evil."

Pankhurst sighed and gulped down a glass of champagne.

"As I said, our country is going down the drain. The values and traditions which made England great are departing with the generation to which we three – and Mr Holmes – belong."

"Surely it can't be that bad," I said.

"I wish you were right," said the officer, screwing up his face. "It is my fault. During my career I did not have time for her; after the death of my dear wife she was raised by her aunt, the wife of my eldest brother. A peculiar woman. So long as she is under the influence of her friends, including our hostess, it is hard to believe."

"I had no idea that Lady Darringford was a feminist," said Holmes.

"She is not actively involved in the movement, but she shares their opinions," said Pankhurst. "By the way, have you met her?"

"As yet we have not had the pleasure."

"She was here a moment ago," he said, looking around. "There she is, heading into the drawing room!"

We looked in the direction he was pointing, but saw only a female silhouette against the backdrop of the illuminated entrance to the villa. I reckoned her to be a lady of medium height with well-rounded hips and a tall coiffure decorated with peacock feathers. She was the first tangible lead to Rupert Darringford, the secretive man with the blood of Minutti and Paolo on his hands.

"We should pay our respects," said Holmes, and as Pankhurst returned to his friends, we detached ourselves from him and left the garden.

"Let us hope that the lady does not share her brother's opinions," I said, remembering the fleeting incident with Darringford in Fulworth.

The detective did not reply. He tried not to lose sight of Lady Alice, who was moving about her house with the natural grace of a swan. Now we finally saw her in full light.

I had to keep my jaw from dropping. Alice Darringford was without doubt the most beautiful woman I had ever seen. She possessed a full feminine figure and light-coloured hair and eyes, which lent her a certain ethereal quality.

She stopped in the middle of the drawing room and clapped her hands.

"Friends, allow me to invite you to a small recital that my dear friend Grace Pankhurst and I have prepared for you!" she called in an enchantingly raspy voice.

The other guests began to return from the garden to the house. The lady made her way to an improvised stage, which until then the orchestra had occupied.

The musicians removed their instruments, leaving only two note stands.

"Grace, my dear, if you would," she said, grasping the violoncello.

Pankhurst's daughter, slim and freckled, brought over her violin and the women patiently waited for the audience to settle down. Thanks to Pankhurst, who rushed in for his daughter's performance and used his elbows to make room for us, we were able to watch the recital unobstructed from the first row.

I immediately recognised the piece. It was Brahms' Concert for Violin and Violoncello. Both women had it rehearsed with endearing precision. It may have lacked lightness of touch, but thanks to the goddess-like presence of Lady Darringford, to me it sounded like the sweetest music from heaven.

The bows slid along the strings with a gracefulness that captivated even Holmes. He closed his eyes and listened with bated breath, as though he feared that his respiration might interrupt the music. The other guests were similarly enraptured, including the morose soldier.

Suddenly a false note crept into the mellifluous tones, then immediately another one. Everyone noticed it. The people began whispering among themselves; they had no idea what was happening. The false note had come from the violin, which tried to continue playing for a moment longer, but then gave up its vain effort.

It fell quiet. Lady Alice frowned and Grace lowered her eyes, crestfallen.

"Forgive me, I have a cramp in my hand," she said, almost in tears.

She vainly tried to make a fist, but the muscle would not budge. She was oppressed by the thought that she had ruined everyone's evening. I felt sorry for her. Pankhurst wanted to console her, but the detective quickly jumped onto the stage and took charge of the unhappy young lady. He gallantly helped her down and kissed her hand.

"Put a compress on it," he advised her.

He too had had experience with cramps caused by holding a bow. Then he delivered Grace to her father, smiled at her kindly, and returned to Lady Darringford.

"It would be a shame to deprive your guests of such beautiful music," he said, picking up Grace's violin. "Would you permit me to accompany you?"

Lady Darringford pursed her lips, raised her eyebrows and looked at him from head to toe.

"It is a difficult piece. Are you a good violinist?"

"More of a talented amateur."

"Very well," she said sweetly. "My friends, your attention please. We will continue!"

The detective bowed, placed the violin under his chin and turned back the pages of the notes to the start of the last movement. He and the lady counted silently to each other and began to play.

The company again listened.

At first everything went smoothly, but then Holmes performed a slight flurry of improvisation. It could be discerned only by those who knew Brahms's piece well, and by Lady Alice.

She shot him a glance, but continued playing. Then she too improvised. She smiled in triumph at how she had managed to momentarily snap the detective out of his concentration. It was terrific. The concert had turned into a contest!

They carried on this game of improvisation for several minutes. Then my friend tightened his grip on the bow and applied it with such vigour to the strings that he began drowning out the violoncello. Out hostess could not let that pass and perfunctorily increased her volume too.

It was delightful!

But not even Holmes's mastery could outshine the sound of the violoncello, at least for me. Both musicians put all they had into the performance. Carried away by passion, their foreheads broke out in sweat. The guests remained hushed as they watched this joust between two artists, for whom music had become a weapon.

The pace quickened, but I saw only the woman.

I listened to the enchanting music and allowed myself to be carried away on its waves somewhere outside time and space.

It was love at first sight.

VIII
Nothing Human...

When Holmes and our hostess finished playing loud applause broke out in the drawing room. In my opinion the ovation was richly deserved, and I also applauded vigorously. Lady Alice and the detective were bowing every which way and my companion was being bombarded with congratulations for saving the unexpected situation.

Lady Darringford extricated herself from the cluster of admirers and shook his hand.

"You were a fine adversary," she said, her bosom heaving.

"I thought that we were playing together, not against one another," said Holmes jovially.

"It depends on how you look at music and the world, Mr. ..."

"Parker, Cedric Parker. And this is my friend, Dr Watson."

"How odd, I immediately figured you for a doctor," said Alice, smiling and looking me directly in the eyes for the first time. "Judging by how you were examining me, I thought you must be either a doctor or a womaniser."

I turned beet red.

"It is all right, you flatter me," she quickly added.

She was about forty, perhaps less, but the smooth skin on her face made any estimate of her exact age a pleasant yet fruitless pursuit. Thanks to her coquettishness I did not even feel much older than she, despite the fact that Holmes and I were old enough to be her father.

Pankhurst pushed his way to us with the contrite Grace.

"Alice, it was wonderful!" cried the girl, hurling her arms around her friend's neck, while the officer greeted Lady Darringoford with a subtle nod of his head. "I was so afraid that I would ruin your performance."

"Fortunately I was able to replace you," said Holmes, returning her violin.

Grace thanked him and took back the instrument, but otherwise did not even look at him. It was peculiar. After all, he had helped her out of a tight spot and had saved the evening.

"How is your hand, my dear?" asked the Lady, placing her arm around the girl's shoulders maternally and leading her young charge away, for all the world as though we had ceased to exist.

"It is better, it was just a momentary indisposition," said the girl, evidently relieved that Lady Alice was not angry with her.

The two women clearly were very close, just as Pankhurst had told us in the garden. I did not see anything amiss, but was unfamiliar with the details and did not know what opinions Lady Darringford could put in Grace's head.

"Are you leaving us, my lady?" the detective asked. "I had hoped that we would have time to speak together."

"My dear Mr Parker, I would also like to get to know you and your kind companion, but you see how many guests I have. It would be rude of me to devote all of my time only to you. You must therefore excuse me now. Why don't you come tomorrow afternoon for tea?"

"It is agreed," said Holmes, accepting the invitation on both our behalves.

Alice Darringford floated off nobly. I followed her with my eyes until her peacock feather disappeared into the crowd.

"She knows how to bewitch a fellow," said Pankhurst conspiratorially. "But don't get your hopes up. That woman has left a trail of broken hearts!"

I felt ashamed that my glances had been so obvious and tried to laugh it off by waving my hand, but Holmes bristled.

"I do not follow your meaning, my dear fellow," he said. "The Lady is certainly admirable, I do not deny it; but to attribute any ulterior motive to us is not gentlemanly of you. Dr Watson is a married man!"

Pankuhrst mumbled something about him not being the only one, but did not continue in this vein further, for which I was thankful.

The officer remained in our company a little while longer and then set off in search of his daughter. We stayed at the party another two hours, but did not encounter the lady again, only spying her here and there as she moved among the other guests.

At around midnight we left and our carriage took us home.

As we shared our impressions of the evening it surprised me that Holmes did not mention Lady Darringford even once. It seemed that Pankhurst's daughter, Grace, had made a bigger impression on him.

But my thoughts remained in the company of the enchanting Alice, so I did not pay much attention to him. I therefore do not have much to relate from the long journey home.

But the detective kept up the topic even after we arrived home.

"An interesting girl, your friend's daughter," he said as we sat in the drawing room sipping cognac.

Did I detect the sound of Aphrodite's angels? As far as I recalled, Holmes, whose priorities had always been elsewhere, had been struck by cupid's arrow only once before. In my eyes Grace Pankhurst could not compare either in beauty or intelligence to the late Irene Adler[18].

But I could not explain the detective's interest in the girl as anything other than a growing affection. She was neither a woman suspected of a crime nor a client.

"In what way did she capture your attention?" I asked deliberately, careful not to step into a wasps' nest.

"As yet I cannot say," he said thoughtfully. "But I will tell you one thing, my friend. That girl certainly conceals more than her father and everyone else thinks."

It sounded serious.

While I had been married several times and had more than once experienced the infatuation that a woman's beauty could cause, Lady Darringford seemed almost like a miracle.

But I would be a poor friend indeed were I to attempt to discourage his burgeoning feelings for a much younger woman. Instead I smiled and drank to his health. Perhaps the sound of the violin had brought two lonely souls together and the reserved way in which Grace had exchanged words with the detective had attracted him.

"And how did Lady Darringford strike you?" I asked.

---

[18] According to W. S. Baring-Gould, Irene Adler, who almost succeeded in outwitting Holmes in the case known as *A Scandal in Bohemia*, was born Clara Stephenson on September 7, 1858 in Trenton, New Jersey, and after a turbulent life died there on October 3, 1903.

"Very well, just like you, Watson," he laughed. "And those words about a trail of broken hearts to her bedroom! Some might take that as a challenge. But she certainly did not behave like a feminist."

He had brought up what the old officer had said, which I had also been pondering.

"Pankhurst is old fashioned, I am sure that he was exaggerating," I said. "He considers any woman who wants to drive her own automobile a feminist. He seems to have forgotten that he has served a queen his whole life. God knows what led him to this opinion. Not every accomplished and self-assured woman is a feminist, after all."

"An impassioned defence! Do make sure that your wife does not find out. She might interpret it the wrong way."

He was right.

For the first time since laying eyes on Lady Darringford I thought of my wife and was beset by a feeling of guilt. I loved her and my feelings for the beautiful Alice seemed like a betrayal. Never mind that it was purely platonic; I knew that given the chance reason would give way to lust.

"Why must you keep bringing that up?" I said angrily, although the anger was mostly directed at myself.

Holmes shrugged his shoulders and did not test me further. He recognised that I alone needed to resolve my inner demons. We each had our own opinions about these matters, but I was encouraged by the last question that he asked me on the staircase as we went up to our rooms.

"What do you think about love? Can it still afflict those as old as us?"

"It is a natural human reaction, one that we should not discourage," I said, and we bade each other goodnight.

Alice Darringford certainly made me feel less than sixty, but I kept that to myself.

***

In the light of day Alice's garden was even more beautiful than at night, and the same could be said of its owner. But that afternoon I had the opportunity to enjoy the former much more closely, as a spring storm was raging outside and our meeting thus took place in the drawing room. All trace of yesterday evening's party was gone. The servants had cleaned up everything and returned the polished furniture in the morning.

Lady Darringford was wearing a long, light-coloured dress and her hair was tied in a braid. The way she sat in the armchair across from us, with her knees firmly pressed together, a handkerchief in one hand and a cup of tea in the other, gave her an air of modesty.

Since our conversation the night before Holmes and I had only exchanged a few words, mainly of a practical nature. That morning we both had been burdened by questions for which neither of us had any answer. The detective seemed distracted. And my resolve to resist Alice's charms was tested every time she looked at me.

But she was in a very fine mood. The garden party evidently had been a great success, thanks in large part to the concert, for which she again thanked Holmes. For about half an hour, while the servant laid out refreshments, we chatted about the unpredictability of May weather and how we were looking forward to the summer. Alice was no fool, however, and after a short while she sensed that we had come for a different purpose.

"Meteorological forecasts are no doubt a classic English topic of conversation over afternoon tea, but something tells me that you are weighed down by other matters," she said simply.

The detective conceded that she was right and stood up from the table. Whenever he was about to interrogate a witness or launch into a monologue he liked to stand up and pace with his arms folded behind his back.

Today he did the same.

But before he started asking questions, he noticed a series of framed photographs of the lady's nearest and dearest displayed on a bureau. Among them were several photographs of Rupert Darringford.

"That is my brother," said our hostess, noticing his inquisitive gaze.

"Brother..." Holmes repeated softly.

Of course he had recognised the man in the photographs, and he examined them with even greater interest. Many were taken in exotic countries: India, Ceylon, Burma and elsewhere. They confirmed what the secret service had told us about his passion for travel. In one of the photographs Lord Darringford posed with a tribe of African natives, a large boa constrictor draped around his neck.

"That must be very dangerous!" said the detective.

"Beautiful things often are," said Alice, her eyes sparkling.

"Does that mean women as well?"

"It depends what woman you have in mind," she answered.

This wordplay evidently amused her.

He picked up another silver-framed photograph in which the siblings could be seen together. Alice was sitting on the hood of the Silver Ghost, while Darringford nonchalantly leaned against the open door. He looked more jovial here then when we had met him. In the background was an old castle, probably in Scotland.

"Our last photograph together," said the lady wistfully.

"The last?"

"Yes, it was taken three years ago. I have not seen my brother since."

"Oh I see," said Holmes.

He stared at the photo for a little while longer and then returned it to its place.

"May I inquire as to what happened?"

Alice placed her cup on the table and dabbed the tears from her eyes with a handkerchief. Talking about her brother upset her. No doubt the siblings had had some sort of falling out. I sat closer to her and tried to comfort her.

"I do not know myself exactly," she sobbed. "He suddenly disappeared and broke off all communication with me."

"Strange."

"The only thing that makes me happy is the knowledge that he is still alive. About twice a year he sends me a letter or telegram, always from a different corner of the globe. You see, Rupert is the only person I have in the world."

"Which makes his behaviour even more curious," said the detective.

"He has been rather queer since childhood," said Alice, sighing. "When our parents died it made things worse. I thought that his wandering and adventurous nature would change things for the better, but clearly the opposite has happened. I would give everything for him to just come home."

"I have heard a rumour that he suffers from a mental illness."

"I would prefer not to talk about that, it is too private and delicate a matter. Yes, he is not healthy, but he is not crazy, as some people say."

"Do you really have no notion of where your brother is now?"

"No," she said, lowering her eyes. "He sent his last telegram from the continent, just before Christmas."

That did not surprise us.

"From Italy?" asked Holmes.

"Yes, how did you know?" said the lady with surprise.

"We recently met there with his... business partners," Holmes coughed, glancing at me quickly. "May I see the telegram?"

"Certainly," said Alice.

She jumped up and took a leather folder tied with a ribbon from the bureau. It contained several telegrams, which she gave us to examine. Holmes looked them over and then handed them to me.

They did not contain anything that could lead us to him. As the lady said, they were all sent from somewhere else around the world. They contained only a few printed words about his health or that he was still not considering coming home, a few orders for the servants and a request to his sister not to try to find him. When the time came he would contact her again.

"These business associates whom you mentioned, they do not know anything about him?" Alice inquired.

"Unfortunately they do not have his address either," said Holmes. "We hoped that we would be able to contact him through you. We need him to confirm a few things."

"I cannot help you with that," said Lady Darringford, wiping away the tears that were running down her round cheeks. "Rupert's whereabouts are just as much a mystery to me as they are to you."

We had accomplished the task for which we had come. I was disappointed that we no longer had a reason to remain in the presence of this gentle creature, but on the other hand it was also a kind of liberation. Were I to remain longer in her company I might not be able to control my infatuation.

"Allow me to ask one last question," said Holmes as we were leaving. "Has your brother ever mentioned the names Minutti or Bollinger?"

"The first of these is unfamiliar to me," said the lady, searching her memory. "By the second do you mean Albert Bollinger? Everyone knows that his sister, Emily, is my good friend. He was last in this house as a guest together with his sister a few weeks ago. Why?"

"I think that your brother came into contact with them recently."

"But Emily certainly would have told me! You must be mistaken."

The detective bowed his head and kissed her on the hand. I must admit that I was slightly jealous; it seemed to me that his lips lingered on the smooth skin of her white hand longer than was strictly necessary. But I immediately expelled such nonsense from my head and chided myself for it. I was acting like a smitten schoolboy.

On the way back to London Holmes was again wrapped in silence, nor was I in the mood to discuss our case. Neither did it surprise me when he perfunctorily asked the coachman to stop on Victoria Street and got out without a word. He only mumbled something about having to stop somewhere due to Miss Pankhurst and that he would only return late in the evening.

Then it was true: his imagination had been captivated by the Pankhurst girl. Well, you can't argue about taste, I said to myself, and drove home.

But the real fun was about to start.

***

I changed into a housecoat, lit the fireplace, poured myself a glass of whiskey and settled into my favourite armchair. I had a lot of paperwork to do in connection with my clinic, which was now being overseen by a medical student. I had not gotten any work done since Holmes's coronary and now seemed like an opportune moment to catch up.

I worked until night fell and the streetlamps came on. At that point the paperwork began to bore me. I put it aside, took up a magazine, and promptly dozed off.

Around nine o'clock I was awoken by the doorbell.

It occurred to me that it must be Holmes. Our housekeeper was on holiday during my wife's absence, so I got up to open the door for my companion.

But instead of the detective I found Alice Darringford.

"Has something happened?" I said with surprise.

"Forgive me for disturbing you at such an hour, but I did not know where else to go," she whispered.

She seemed disturbed. Her eyes gazed wildly from side to side and she was trembling all over.

I could not leave her standing at the doorway. A female visitor while my wife was away would certainly attract a great deal of attention in our street full of curious eyes. But I did not want to turn her away. I apologised for my informal attire and invited her in.

I directed her to the drawing room and bid her sit on a comfortable sofa at the fireplace.

"From the moment when you left yesterday afternoon I cannot rid myself of these feelings," she whispered, wringing her hands nervously. "I must always think of my brother. Mr Parker's questions upset me greatly."

"I understand," I said nodding, and sat down next to her.

Having her near me, so defenceless and seeking comfort, made my heart beat furiously. My mouth was dry and I had to drink some water in order to be able to speak.

"It occurred to me that as a doctor you could give me something to calm my nerves," she continued. "My personal doctor is away on holiday and I would rather not share my family problems with a complete stranger."

"Of course, I am glad to be of service!" I assured her.

I brought her a calming pill from my medical bag and placed it in her open palm.

She looked at me thankfully with her large eyes, which shone in the light of the fire. Then she blinked and turned away from the light.

"Forgive me, my head is pounding," she said, putting the back of her hand on her forehead.

I immediately dimmed the lamps.

"Is that better?"

"Yes," she said, sighing.

The room was immersed in romantic shadows. Everything was right for me to reveal my feelings to her.

But I remained steadfast. In spite of her beauty I would not threaten my marriage to satisfy short-term lust. In the depths of my soul I knew that my infatuation was nothing more than that.

But Lady Darringford chose to ignore my official union. She suddenly turned towards me and passionately kissed me!

Instinctively I returned her embrace.

IX
One Woman for Two Men

I was in heaven for about sixty seconds, although it seemed like much longer. When Alice Darringford's lips met mine the world around me ceased to exist. Everything fell silent. The room seemed to float far away from my conscious awareness, together with my resolve not to succumb to the lady's allure.

Never have I experienced a sweeter kiss. Alice smelled like a mixture of exotic scents, which pervaded my nose up to my brain, where they burned an indelible trail, while her white and silky hands played with my hair. She slid her fingers over my neck, caressing and kneading it with her hands, running over my Adam's apple, and sometimes pressing it so that I almost ceased breathing. There was something so unbelievably exciting about this that I shuddered and trembled. I would not have believed that at my age I could experience something so intense.

In my ecstasy I did not hear the door opening or the footsteps leading to the drawing room. I only came to my senses when I heard a loud outraged gasp.

The lady, sitting with her back to the door, felt the presence of someone else in the room and broke away from me. But it was vain to pretend that nothing had happened. We had been caught *in flagranti*.

"Watson!" cried Holmes, holding a dossier in his hands. "What is the meaning of this?"

I froze and extracted myself from the woman's grasp. My guilty cheeks were blushing, confirmation of our loss of reason.

The detective was frowning like an angry judge and he measured us with an aggrieved look. A black cloud formed over me. My moral credit was shot, as much as though I had been caught by my wife.

"I should probably go," said Alice after a pause, in which I searched for an answer, but only managed to gape.

She did not expect me or my companion to object, but only smiled with confusion, fixed her hair and brushed past Holmes to the door. He did not say a word to her or so much as look in her eyes. In fact, he looked away.

When the door shut behind her an embarrassing silence descended on the drawing room broken only by the crackling of the wood burning in the fireplace and the distant din of the street.

Then I grew angry.

An adult man, his face wrinkled by experience, who has seen and lived through so much, is never happy to find himself in the position of a chastised schoolboy. I alone was responsible for my behaviour, and I alone had to deal with its consequences. Holmes may have meant well, but his actions crossed the line of what I was prepared to tolerate. It was not his place to play the moralist. I decided to go on the offensive and tell him so in no uncertain terms.

"We are both adults and I do not owe you an explanation," I said.

Holmes, who was still standing in the doorway, levelled his steely eyes on me with such a stony glare that I nearly shook.

"I had no idea you were such a cynic," he barked, clenching the stack of papers even tighter.

"What is cynical about my feelings for Lady Darringford?" I said, defending myself. "Of course I am married, but please leave these matters up to me. I can fully devote myself to our investigation."

"Do not play the innocent! You acted against all principle! I confided my feelings for Lady Alice to you, even that I might be in love with her. I told you that I saw her reserved nature as a challenge, and she herself has indicated that I should try to win her! You acted like a friend, but only to stick the knife in my back and seduce the woman at the first opportunity!"

Now it was my turn to stare with astonishment.

"Excuse me?" I said. "But you were not talking about Lady Darringford! At least, that is not how I understood it! I thought that the woman you were talking about was..."

He did not even let me finish and lifted his hand in front of my face.

"Silence!" he shouted.

He slowly lowered his hand and his cold look turned into something worse: disdain. God as my witness, it was a horrible mistake.

"When did I stop knowing you?"

"For God's sake, Holmes, you know that I would never knowingly do that to you!"

He shook his head.

"You betrayed my trust, and even worse, my friendship," he whispered in a parched voice, turning his back to me. "I am disappointed, Watson."

I did not know what to say.

Holmes was finished. I was not even worth looking at anymore. He collected himself and went without another word upstairs to his room. His heavy footsteps sounded on the staircase like the death knoll of our long friendship.

**

I prescribed myself sleeping pills, but they only half helped. I spent the night in a delirium of terrible nightmares and hallucinations. I awoke drenched in sweat, with the knowledge that the bad dreams reflected the cruel reality that my life was collapsing like a house of cards.

How could I have been so stupid? But the whole morning I only stared dully at the ceiling. I did not have the courage to leave the room and meet Holmes.

At least it gave me time to think about what had happened and why. Of course I easily understood why he had fallen in love with Lady Alice. Her intelligence and charm rivalled that of Irene Adler, and she was much more Holmes's type than Grace Pankhurst. The idea that the detective may have fallen for that girl all at once seemed laughable and twisted. How could the thought have even occurred to me?

I thought too about my own actions. I now considered my relationship with Alice a closed chapter. I would not sacrifice my marriage on the altar of a senseless infatuation and I hoped that my wife would never find out about this incident.

I could not, however, understand what attraction I held for Alice, a man so many years her senior. Intelligence, social position, experience, maturity? These were qualities that she would surely admire more in Holmes.

In addition, her behaviour did not fit with what my old friend the officer had said during the garden party. Perhaps the stories about the broken hearts of her admirers were just gossip whispered by bored aristocrats? In any case, the Lady was still unmarried and unattached, which again did not fit with her beauty and social position.

I considered all of the possibilities, but none of them seemed the right one.

I felt empty and sore. What would I do if I lost my best and oldest friend? And all due to a misunderstanding, a failure in judgement, and my rash impetuousness.

Just before noon the doors banged in the hallway and I heard the detective go downstairs and leave the house. I could now descend and have breakfast. But I was not the least bit hungry, and just ate some coffee and biscuits.

I was tempted to spend the whole day in my housecoat, but finally decided to do what I would have advised any of my patients who came to me similarly depressed: I got dressed and went into town.

Aimlessly I wandered through the streets, sat for a while in Regent's Park and watched the people go by; ladies with parasols and gentlemen in straw hats, drawn outdoors by the beautiful weather. But nothing could cheer me or distract me from my melancholy and all-consuming guilt. For all I cared it could start raining.

I increasingly began to recognise that there was only one solution to this unpleasant situation. I had to explain everything to Holmes rationally and continue on in our investigation, which the detective was no doubt presently engaged in without me. Reconciliation was now my chief aim.

I ate lunch in a restaurant on Russel Square and slowly headed home.

It was quiet in the house. I gathered up all my courage and went up to Holmes's room. I hoped that he would be at home. I wanted to find him in a mood in which we could talk.

But he was gone.

The room was impeccably tidy. I recognised that he had been there during the day; on the table he had left a plate with unfinished lunch, but he had once again left.

On the bureau was the dossier that he had brought back with him the evening before. It lay open and several yellowed pieces of paper were visible within. On the title page Holmes had written "Pankhurst" in black ink.

So the detective's interest in young Grace persisted. But if not love, what guided him?

I took the dossier to the drawing room and settled into my favourite armchair in front of the fireplace. But today I would not under any circumstances open the door for Lady Alice.

I opened a bottle of wine and began to read.

To my surprise the file was not about Grace, but about Richard Marsden Pankhurst. Although the notorious left-wing attorney and politician had been dead these past thirteen years, I remembered him well, thanks mainly to his radical opinions, chief among them home rights for Ireland, Indian independence, the dissolution of the Anglican Church and liquidation of the House of Lords, all of which led to him being dubbed the Red Doctor. Although he was never elected to parliament, his controversial vision of the world gained him respect among the

Independent Labour Party and his legacy lived on long after his sudden death[19].

I also learned from Holmes's notes that he was the cousin of my old friend Harry Pankhurst, Grace's father.

"Again the connections escape me, my friend," I whispered under my breath and sipped my wine. It was good and strong, perhaps a little too strong. In any case, the detective had managed to fog over the reason why he was so interested in the Pankhurst family.

I returned to reading in the hope that the next lines would reveal the solution to this riddle.

But all I found was a flood of seemingly unrelated information. Richard Pankhurst had founded the National Society for the Support of Women's Suffrage and had authored a bill that became the Act on Property of Married Women in 1882, giving wives absolute control over their property and profits.

He married Emmeline Goulden[20], an activist twenty years his junior, with whom he formed the Women's Rights League. He belonged to the same political circle as George Bernard Shaw. Emmeline Goulden-Pankhurst, who after her husband's death founded the Women's Social and Political

---

[19] Richard Marsden Pankhurst (1834–1898) was a lawyer. He was born in Stoke but spent most of his life in Manchester and London. Known as the Red Doctor, he sought election to parliament, first in 1883 as a candidate for Manchester, then in 1885 in Kent, each time unsuccessfully. He died suddenly at the age of 64 due to a stomach ulcer.

[20] Emmeline Pankhurst (1858–1928) was one of the founders of the Women's Social and Political Union. Her name is connected with the fight for women's rights in the period leading up to the First World War.

Union, a militant suffragette movement, was without a doubt the aunt who had raised Grace Pankhurst.

Now I was beginning to understand where Holmes was headed. He feared that under the influence of her aunt Grace would take up the violent methods of the suffragettes, which had been escalating in intensity for several years, and I dare say had made them a threat to the very fabric of society.

He certainly did not want Lady Alice to become embroiled in leftist radicalism, especially as she was torn away from her brother and was groping for something to give meaning to her life. Hence her interest in Grace. From the start Holmes had been interested Grace's influence over Lady Darringford, not the other way around! How blind I had been to confuse it with love and to overlook his real feelings for Alice!

In a state of agitation I finished my glass of wine and discovered that in the course of my reading I had managed to drink the whole bottle. I still had a few pages to read and the feeling of guilt still had not left me.

I went to fetch another bottle and continued along the trail of Holmes's thoughts. The dossier also contained files about the participation of the Pankhursts in the Bloody Sunday riot in Trafalgar Square on November 13, 1887.

I remembered it well.

The long period of crisis that began in 1873 and lasted almost until the end of the century created difficult social conditions in Britain and similar economic malaise in the Irish countryside. Falling food prices led to unemployment, which resulted in a great internal migration. Workers moved by the thousands to the cities, where they crippled the labour market, and devalued their working conditions and wages. As often happens in British politics, the problems in Ireland were also reflected in a number of domestic affairs. In November 1887 there were demonstrations by unemployed workers from London's East End. Their daily conflicts with the police regularly made headlines.

Trafalgar was the symbolic place where the working class met the middle class from West End. This captured the attention of the small but growing socialist movement. The police and government attempts to put pressure on the demonstrators only served to energise the radical wing of the Liberal party and activists for free speech, who saw the square as a public space, necessary for public as well as political use.

To my understanding the closeness of British and Irish radicalism was also due to the fact that the working classes in English cities were often made up of a large number of native Irishmen. London as well as the industrial areas of northern England had a large number of Irish workers, concentrated in the East End, where they competed with other groups, such as the wave of Jews arriving from Eastern Europe. Among the recent arrivals the Irish and the Jews were the most beset by unemployment. And then there was the international dimension: the workers made common cause with the fate of the anarchists arrested after the Haymarket riots in Chicago the previous year. The hanging of four of them on November 11 indeed led to the demonstration, which turned into Bloody Sunday.

I could see it as clearly as though it were yesterday.

Some ten thousand people marched to Trafalgar Square from several directions, led by Elizabeth Reynolds, John Burns, Annie Besant and Robert Cunningham-Graham, the leaders of the Social-Democratic Federation. With them marched George Bernard Shaw, who made a speech.

Two thousand policemen and four hundred soldiers were on hand to suppress the demonstration. The skirmishes that broke out between them and the marchers, including women and children, led to the first acts of violence. Hundreds of workers were injured and at least three of them succumbed to their wounds. In the end there were even more dead and wounded. Two hundred people needed medical treatment; many others never made it to hospital, either out of fear of arrest or simply because they could not afford the fees. Most of the injuries were caused by the fists and truncheons of the police.

It was fortunate that more people did not lose their lives that day, as both the infantry and the cavalry were present. The soldiers who defended their positions with bayonets were not allowed to open fire and the cavalry were ordered to keep their sabres sheathed.

Bloody Sunday remained an important milestone in the modern history of the British and Irish left. It kick-started public interest in the *social question*, represented mainly by the appalling living conditions of the poor in the East End. But the murders of Jack the Ripper, which took place in the period shortly thereafter, distracted the press, which always focused on sex and violence, best of all in combination with each other.

At the bottom of the page Holmes had written two names followed by a question mark: Darringford and Bollinger.

Did it refer to Rupert or Alice Darringford?

My vision was starting to blur under the influence of the strong wine. My eyelids began to shut and I was no longer able to focus on the letters. I leaned my head back for a moment and involuntarily fell asleep, for all the world like the worst drunkard.

I awoke only the next day at daybreak.

The back of my neck ached and my spine was stiff from the night spent in the chair. My breath smelled of alcohol. The fire had long ago gone out, but someone had thrown a warm blanket over my legs.

Had my wife returned? Or had Holmes decided to take pity on me?

As though my thoughts had beckoned him, at that moment the detective stepped into the room.

I could not say, however, that his expression had become any more agreeable since our argument.

"Get up, Watson," he said. "It is time to settle the score."

X
Cosi fan tutte

Holmes sent me upstairs to get dressed and put myself in order. I felt as though I were preparing myself for the grave. Meanwhile he waited for me in the drawing room, dressed and ready to depart. I could only guess where he wanted to go so early in the morning. Perhaps to a pistol duel somewhere in the plains outside the city?

When I returned to the drawing room I noticed that the detective was clearing away the remains of my drunken night. He had taken away the bottle of wine and my glass, folded the blanket, picked up the scattered sheets of his dossier and cleaned the fireplace.

"That took you a while," he complained, grasping me around the shoulder. "It is high time we get going. Soon it will be nine o'clock and ideally everything should be cleared up before noon. Let's go, they are waiting for us."

He led me out of the house to a carriage that was standing at the curb. To my surprise it contained Mycroft. Was he Holmes's second? He greeted me sullenly and motioned me to sit next to him. The detective took the seat across from us and we set off.

Curiosity got the better of me.

"Where are we going?" I asked.

My friend turned from the window and sighed.

"As I already said: It is time to end this story."

"What in God's name are you talking about?" I cried, imagining the ridiculous spectacle of a duel to the death. "Do you really want to bury our friendship this way?"

He looked at me as though it was I who had lost my mind. Then the light of understanding appeared in his eyes and the pupils sparkled.

"My dear Watson, I really do owe you an explanation; in all this haste I did not realise it," he said laughing. "I have succeeded in solving our case and now we are on our way to confront the criminal."

"Really?" I cried with surprise. "You are no longer angry at me because of Lady Alice?"

"Nor can I be," he said, shrugging his shoulders. "I have a confession, my friend. That scene the day before yesterday when I berated you, it was all a ruse."

I could not believe my ears!

"It all served only one purpose: My enemies had to be certain that the seeds of discord had been planted between us. Your weakness for women certainly came in handy. But the rest was pure fiction."

"And what role did poor Lady Alice play in all of this?" I asked.

"The central one, my dear friend, indeed the title role."

He did not elaborate further, assuring me that by and by I would learn the true purpose of this drama.

Mycroft, who had been listening to us, smacked his lips and shook his head warily. We all plunged into silent expectation. I was relieved that all had been resolved between us and I spent the rest of the journey looking out the window.

Soon I realised where we were going, which confused me even more.

After several miles the carriage stopped in front of Alice Darringford's villa.

The detective whispered something to his brother, who looked at his watch as though he were expecting someone else to arrive. He remained seated in the vehicle while Holmes and I got out. I was curious to discover what would happen.

An unpleasant maid with grey hair tied up in a tight bun opened the door for us. She tersely asked us what we wanted, holding the door open just a few inches. As we had not been announced, there was nothing to do but act in a manner somewhat unbefitting a gentleman.

Holmes stuck the tip of his shoe in the door and pushed the woman inside before she could slam it shut. He pulled me in with him, through the vestibule and up one of the staircases to the private quarters.

"What are you doing!" the maid cried angrily. "Get out of here! Criminals! Thieves! I will call the police!"

"Call them," said my companion, continuing up the stairs. "It will make my job easier."

I was at the mercy of events and could only observe with astonishment what was happening around me. When we reached the upper floor the detective looked around, not knowing where to go. The hallway decorated with pictures and covered in a thick burgundy carpet led in several possible directions. Luckily Lady Alice suddenly emerged from one of the rooms with a startled expression on her face.

"What is that noise?" she yelled at the frenzied maid, who was mobilising the gardener and the cook downstairs. When the Lady saw us her confusion mounted and she leaned her head to the side with an elegant motion. Even in this state of agitation she was heart-achingly beautiful.

"I know that our visit is unexpected, which makes it all the more pressing," Holmes assured her. "Call off your dogs; we will not be here long."

Lady Darringford hesitated for a moment, glancing back with confusion into the room from which she had just emerged.

"Mr Parker and Doctor Watson," she mumbled. "To what do I owe the pleasure of this ambush?"

"We must talk," said Holmes.

The lady gathered herself and in a dignified manner waved to us to follow her inside. We found ourselves in a study. One wall was lined with a massive bookshelf, decorated with valuable prints, arranged in the shelves up to the ceiling. In front of the bookshelf was a step ladder with wheels. In the middle of the study was a large and polished desk with an ink-well. An open window faced the garden. On the writing pad lay an unfinished letter.

The maid finally fell silent and withdrew with her minions.

Alice sat down and waited, without even offering us coffee. She made it perfectly clear that this involuntary audience should be as short as possible.

"Gentlemen, you are always welcome guests in this house, but today I must ask you to be brief," she said sweetly.

Those eyes, I thought to myself, who could resist them?

My companion did not hurry. He considered, seeking the right words with which to begin, and then exclaimed:

"Few embody such an unpleasant surprise for me as you, Lady Alice."

Since the morning I had been bowled over by a series of reversals, but the wave of astonishment which now poured over me was incomparably greater. Our hostess turned red with anger.

"Pardon me! Are you talking about what you witnessed between me and Dr Watson? Gentlemen, gentlemen, I do not have time today for these foolish games!"

I also felt the need to defend her.

"Holmes, you should apologise!"

But the detective was only getting started.

"You are a liar!" he cried. "Behind the face of an angel lies one of the greatest and most dangerous intriguers that I have ever encountered! But your game is up! I know everything, and I will not let you win!"

Alice's face clouded over and her eyes flared with something that I had never expected to see in them: pure, malignant hatred. But she instantly regained her composure and her plump face contorted into a polite, neutral smile.

But her self-assurance was broken.

"I do not know what you mean," she said defiantly. "In any case, you should go."

"I am not yet finished, my dear," said Holmes sternly. "If I were you I would enjoy my last moments of liberty. Now you will listen to me and cooperate; it is the only way to mitigate your punishment!"

She drummed her fingers on the table top, cast her eyes about the room, and sat down obediently. She appeared willing to listen to him. I held my breath in anticipation.

"Punishment for what?" she asked.

Holmes laughed sharply. "The mask of naivety does not become you, Lady Darringford!"

He was wrong. In my opinion Alice was bewitching in anything, even a potato sack.

"What is my offence then, this crime that you are raving about? Could it be because your friend had the chance to kiss me and you did not..."

That was unfair.

But her taunt slid off the detective like a pea hitting a smooth wall.

"Oh, your attempt to complicate my investigation by driving a wedge between myself and this good fellow Watson is the least of your contemptuous deeds!"

I do not like to be spoken of in this way. I have never quite lost the feeling that the moniker "good fellow" is synonymous with someone who is not particularly clever or perceptive.

"You must have realised that I was on your trail, which is why you trained your feminine guns on me," he continued. "I let on that you had succeeded, but your calibre is laughably small compared with the only woman who has ever succeeded in stirring me! I only regret that I was compelled to let you assault my friend and act as though I did not see it!"

Had I really become a mere weapon for Alice and Holmes to use against each other? It was not agreeable for me to watch them lash their tongues at one another and behave as though I did not exist.

"Get to the point," Alice sputtered, folding her hands in her lap.

"Very well," said the detective. "You are guilty of criminal conspiracy and complicity in the murders that you planned with your brother!"

127

I blinked with surprise. How could that be? What had given Holmes such an idea? How had he deduced it? From the way Alice trembled, however, it was clear that, as always, my companion was not mistaken.

"I told you that my brother disappeared and that I have not seen him in several years!"

"Nevertheless, that is in direct contradiction with the photograph in your drawing room."

"I do not understand..."

"You claim that your brother has been abroad for three years. Indeed, he travels a great deal. I myself have had the privilege of receiving a souvenir from one of his exotic journeys: he tried to poison me with Indian tobacco."

Holmes paused and then revealed the first of his trump cards.

"But that photograph of the two of you must have been taken last year in the autumn! Judging by the weather I would say in late November or early December. That particular type of automobile with which you are photographed, the Silver Ghost, only began to be manufactured last spring. He could not have purchased it earlier!"

"I do not understand such things," she said waving her hand. "I repeat that I do not see my brother. And if he is guilty of any of the things that you claim, it is none of my affair. Is there anything else?"

"There certainly is," said the detective, smiling. "Your protégées."

"My protégées?"

"Grace Pankhurst, for instance, and your other friends from the feminist league."

128

"What is wrong with being a feminist? Are you one of these chauvinists who think that women ought to stay at home and forsake all participation in public life or governance over their own existence?"

"Not at all, I can assure you," said Holmes. "I have nothing against feminism. But you, my dear lady, are not merely a feminist; you are a suffragette, and of the most radical and militant sort!"

"And how did you figure that out?" she barked.

Their conversation was becoming louder and more aggressive.

"For the last two days, during which my friend was alternately floating on a romantic cloud or wallowing in deep depression, I studied your past."

Even under her make-up Alice's beautiful complexion grew slightly pale.

"You know nothing about me!"

"Enough to make a picture of you," the detective retorted. "According to the police records, when you were twenty years old you took part in the Bloody Sunday demonstration. Was it there that you met Mrs Pankhurst, a left-wing activist and suffragette, whose niece you are so fond of?"

"I was a child then, confused by the times. The fact that I know somebody does not mean that I share their opinions!"

"Indubitably. But by all accounts, in addition to the Pankhursts you are friendly with a number of other much more ambiguous sorts, people suspected of radicalism."

Alice Darringford again stood up erect. Her pride had been injured.

"Mr Parker, I am a noblewoman from an old and wealthy family. Why in heaven's name would I take up leftist ideas and opinions that deny my very position in society?"

He shrugged.

"I admit that your motivation is not yet entirely obvious. Logic, deduction and the information from my sources nevertheless speak clearly. There are many clues in this case and they all lead to you. You pull the strings in the secret militant wing of the suffragettes, which carried out this devilish plan!"

"You flatter me and overestimate my abilities," said Alice, laughing. "You are just clutching at straws."

"A plan," Holmes continued, "which aims to concentrate the power of arms manufacturers across Europe into your hands!"

"Why would I want to do that?"

"Money," said the detective, "but mainly to gain influence for the suffragettes and their political goals. You intend to take England hostage. In our turbulent times, politicians will listen to an organisation that wields the reins of a vital industry more than they would a few bitter women."

"Bah! If it was not so laughable I would be insulted," said Alice.

Indeed she resisted the detective's attacks very stout-heartedly. I myself, who had boundless trust in Holmes, was suddenly in doubt about whether perhaps he was mistaken. But I preferred to remain silent.

"You and your brother started inconspicuously enough. You obtained the military secrets of Vito Minutti, except that was not enough; you wanted to control the whole factory. When he did not sell it to you, you killed him. Not with your own hands, mind you, but those of members of the movement. Those zealots would stop at nothing, not even murder!"

"Yes, and we also caused the famine in the sixteenth century," she snapped angrily.

"Do you have any idea how unnecessary that murder was? In time the factory would have fallen into your hands anyway. I learned about your brother by a cheque that he left at Pastor Barlow's."

"Nonsense!"

"As soon as you discovered that the suspicious industrialist had managed to ask Sherlock Holmes for help you decided to get rid of him as well. There is no longer any need to keep up this charade. You of course realised long ago that Mr Parker's beard conceals the face that you wanted to see six feet under."

The Lady rolled her eyes.

"Did I say that your deductions were entertaining? In fact they are boring me."

"Of course you did not carry out the murder yourself; your noble hands are without stain," the detective persisted. "For that you have your comrades. And as soon as you had Minutti's company under your control it was Lord Bollinger's turn."

"I will not listen to any more of this!"

Alice rose to leave, but Holmes blocked her way.

"He was introduced to you by his own sister, your good friend, who is sympathetic to your movement," he shouted. "The poor woman doubtless had no idea that she was sending him to his grave. You seduced him just as you tried to seduce me and Watson! And during one of his visits, when you already had all of his company's secrets in your pocket, you had him killed!

131

Now you control the unsuspecting Emily Bollinger just as you do Minutti's factory through Luigi Pascuale. There is no need to deny it. Confess!"

I felt like one of the mute characters in a moving picture.

Lady Darringford angrily tried to push Holmes aside, and when she failed she hit his chest with her tiny fists. He caught her by the wrist and easily kept her at bay. She howled with rage, but in a moment her sounds turned into muffled laughter. Then she fell around Holmes's neck and laughed uproariously.

"Gentlemen, well done," she said through tears of laughter. "You almost had me. For a moment I thought you were serious. Is this your revenge, doctor?"

"You killed them," said Holmes flatly, releasing her from his grasp. "Either with your own hands or by order. The game is up, Lady Darringford."

She stopped laughing, slowly wiped her eyes and fixed her hair.

"Very well then," she said. "You wanted to keep me at bay with your phantasmagoria, but you have only driven yourself into a corner. Everything you say is nonsense."

"Indeed?"

"Yes. Perhaps you have something on my brother, and I do hope you find him. But as for me and your little theory about the death of Albert Bollinger, who you say I murdered in this very house, you are missing the most important thing."

"Which is?"

"Proof!" she cried triumphantly. "As far as I know Albert is missing, which does not mean dead. And if his body is not found, you will have no proof. No judge or police officer will believe any of your lies."

132

Holmes considered and nodded his head.

"Indeed, without a body my theory is just a weak scaffolding built on clues."

The Lady smiled victoriously and I felt embarrassed. If this was meant to be the end and my friend hoped that she would confess under the burden of his bold accusations, he had come off rather badly. We had only succeeded in embarrassing ourselves, revealing Holmes's disguise, and discrediting our whole investigation. I felt even worse than I had yesterday.

But the detective had still not played his last trump card.

"Then there is nothing left for me to do except search for the lord's body," he said, winking at me conspiratorially.

"You can do so by heading out the door," said Alice frostily. "But do not return without a search warrant. Not that you will obtain one on the basis of these hallucinations, old man."

She waved a contemptuous hand at Holmes's grey hair. He raised his eyebrows slightly and levelled her with a condescending, even regretful look.

"May I suggest you look out the window," he said. "The weather is so fine and your garden so inviting."

She looked at him searchingly and peered out the window.

"What are they doing?!" she cried. "Keep them away from my flower beds!"

I looked over her shoulder out the window. A cordon of uniformed police officers was marching across the beautiful garden. So Mycroft had been waiting for them! Some of the officers carried spades and were looking around, not knowing where to start digging.

133

"You have no right to search the garden!" Alice fumed. "What do you think you will find? A dead body? Do you want to dig up the whole place? That would take you years!"

"The whole garden? No," laughed Holmes, joining us at the window. "Gentlemen! Did you not hear the lady? Get away from those flower beds! And if I see anyone damaging the lawn with their spade they will have to answer to me!"

The sergeant saluted obediently and drove his men away from the flowers.

"Do you see that beech grove and gazebo?" said the detective pointing to the back corner of the garden. "There are newly planted rhododendrons. Dig beneath them and you will find a dead body. Let me know when you do!"

The police officers headed towards the trees. Holmes closed the window and turned towards the room.

The Lady's expression had transformed. Her adorability was gone, replaced by fear and anger. We had hit the button on the nose. I no longer had any doubt that under the trees we would find what Holmes expected.

"It was not very difficult; one need only be familiar with basic natural science," he explained pedantically. "During our walk in the garden the other evening the doctor and I discovered those bushes, which do not at all match the character of the otherwise carefully designed garden. They no doubt weren't a part of the architect's plans. They serve an entirely different purpose. What's more, old men like me, who have sufficient free time for study, know that the roots of beech trees release a poisonous substance into the soil."

The accused woman bit her lower lip.

"Is it dawning on you?" he continued. "Yes, the trees prevent weeds and other competitors taking water from them. But someone tried very hard to make something grow next to these trees. Under other circumstances it would have been a successful attempt at camouflage."

We could hear shovels and pickaxes under the window. The body would not be buried deep.

Lady Darringford was breathing heavily.

"As soon as I got the warning that someone was snooping around in Venice I knew it was you," she said, her face clouding. "Of course I realised that the poisoning and theatrical funeral of the great Sherlock Holmes was a ruse. As soon as you showed up here in that ridiculous disguise everything was clear! You never were able to drop dead in time!"

"Such strong words from such delicate lips," said the detective. "Come come now."

"My brother and that pastor are idiots for not seeing through you," she continued. "One is always better off doing something oneself. And you know what? I strangled Bollinger with my own hands! His Adam's apple just crunched! The doctor knows how dextrous I am with my fingers."

Her confession, uttered with such coldblooded cruelty, and addressed to my ears, threw me into despair. I remembered how her hands had caressed my neck. What would have happened had my friend not intervened?

"Enough talk," said Holmes, defending me. "You can tell this to the police and the judge. I hope you show enough remorse to avoid being sent straight to the gallows!"

But she did not falter.

"You pathetic fool! You have no idea who I am and what is waiting for all of you! You will burn in hell!"

Laughing contemptuously she lunged towards the bookshelf before the detective could stop her.

From behind two volumes she pulled something that looked like a stick of dynamite and waved it in front of us. We covered our heads expecting an explosion, but she just cackled as she broke the stick and tossed it in front of us. A cloud of pungent smoke rose up, filling the room and blinding us.

We heard the doors close behind her, the key clicking in the lock, and her surprisingly rapid footsteps as she ran cackling down the hallway. Holmes groped through the smoke and tried in vain to open the door.

"Did she lock us in?" I called to him.

"Yes," he answered from behind the veil of smoke, which was gradually beginning to dissipate.

But in those few second she had succeeded in getting away.

When the smoke faded I looked across the room and saw Holmes silently staring at the door through which she had disappeared with a sad expression on his face.

"*Cosi fan tutte*,"[21] he sighed.

---

[21] Italian: "Thus do they all." Also the name of an opera by Mozart. Holmes is no doubt referring to the fact that the incomparable Irene Adler also ran away from him in *A Scandal in Bohemia*.

XI
Intermezzo

The black cloud of smoke in Lady Darringford's study had dissipated. But in that short time it had paralysed not only our vision but also our ability to move. As soon as Holmes understood that we were imprisoned inside the room he lunged towards the window, opened it and from his jacket pocket pulled out a whistle. The sound alarmed the policemen, who were pulling up shrubs and turf from the beech grove and digging with their shovels in the dirt. Now they looked up at the window from which smoke was billowing.

"She got away!" he shouted. "Search the house! She must not escape!"

The sergeant bellowed orders. He left two men at the pit while the rest ran towards the house. I feared that they would not be able to surround the villa in time. Then I was overcome by a fit of coughing and had to again prop myself up against the parapet.

Mycroft, alarmed by the smoke and the whistling, also ran into the garden. A glance at the garden and the two of us standing helplessly at the window told him everything he needed to know.

"Are you all right?" he called.

"She has only injured our pride," said Holmes.

"What happened?"

"She locked us in the study and escaped. I have already issued instructions."

"Very well. Wait there, I am coming for you!"

As we did not know how to walk on walls this command was rather unnecessary.

In a few minutes we heard Mycroft's heavy footsteps behind the door.

"Brother, are you still there?"

We assured him that indeed we were and he called two men over to break down the door. After the second strike the wood gave way and we were free.

The hallway was full of policemen running from room to room, shaking their heads.

The news was bad.

"Lady Darringford has disappeared without a trace," said Mycroft gloomily.

"How is that possible?"

"My men were only watching the main entrance. We did not anticipate that she would resist arrest, especially since the garden was full of police. The Lady escaped through the cellar and servants' entrance together with the housekeeper and other domestics. The house is completely empty."

Indeed, the vestibule beneath the staircase contained only two despondent agents in civilian dress.

Holmes fixed them with his penetrating gaze. But there was no point upbraiding them.

"Back to work," he said. "Whatever direction she has headed she has no doubt left clues."

"Now it's just a matter of finding them," Mycroft sighed.

"Do not fear. We have come very far and I still have strength enough to continue the chase," said my companion.

We returned to Alice's study, which had been aired out. How many clues did it hide?

Books, letters in the desk, all could contain valuable information.

On the desk lay the letter which Lady Alice had been writing when we interrupted her. Holmes headed straight for it.

He read the first lines and smiled softly.

"It is a kind of written confession," he said. "A letter to a certain Jacques in which the Lady discusses plans for their upcoming nuptials."

"Alice wants to get married?"

"So it seems. According to this letter the wedding is planned for this autumn."

"But I thought she never wanted to marry!"

"No doubt it is merely a marriage of convenience, Watson," he said, rummaging through the other papers on the desk until he found the envelope. "Yes, I was right. The addressee is Jacques Picard, a leading French industrialist."

"May I hazard a guess that he manufactures weapons?" I said.

"Precisely," replied Holmes. "Lady Alice was acquiring control over the war machinery very meticulously. She planned to marry this arms manufacturer, but I do not expect that the marriage was meant to last long. The poor fellow would have been a mere instrument serving her aims; our praying mantis would have disposed of him just as she did the others. Most ingenious and cruel!"

"We should warn him," said Mycroft, taking the envelope from Holmes.

"I will leave that to you, brother. Nevertheless, now that we have uncovered her plans, Lady Darringford will have much less room to operate. I do not think that Mr Picard will be hearing from his fiancée in the near future. I suppose that you will issue an immediate warrant for her arrest. And as for Bollinger and Pascuale, *sans* her they are just like empty cartridges without a detonator."

"But as long as she is free she will surely continue to plot and intrigue," said Mycroft. "She knows our strategic plans and secret materials, for which Kaiser Wilhelm would give anything, and can blackmail us. That woman will not give up so easily. She must be rendered toothless!"

As I listened to them the whole truth finally sunk in. Alice had been revealed as a radical feminist who would stop at nothing and who was ready to sacrifice human lives for her twisted ideals. Her behaviour gave the term suffragette a completely different meaning.

After all, the suffragettes were originally middleclass women, for the most part unmarried, frustrated by their social situation and economic condition. In their radical actions they sought a path to change. Their feeling of powerlessness led to a movement that inspired thousands of women to fight for the right to vote.

Soon they took direct action, tying themselves to railway tracks, starting fires in post boxes and trash bins, and breaking windows and display cases. They even set off bombs. Many went on hunger strikes and had to be fed by force. But they certainly would not condone what Alice had done.

Which was another reason why Lady Darringford did not seem to fit into this group. She was born wealthy and had an excellent position in society. Hence her motives remained a mystery.

140

While I pondered thus my companions were examining the bookshelf.

Just as I had expected Holmes found much of interest in it. In particular he was intrigued by a peculiar family album, resembling a book, which he pulled out of the shelf and began to leaf through.

As we could see by the date indicated in gold letters in the blood red leather of the cover, the album was put together about a year ago. Instead of photographs, Alice had filled it with articles and news clippings, probably from stories in which she had played a large part. There were short notices about various accidents that had befallen people whose names were unfamiliar to me. But the detective recognised the names of important figures in European industry. Other pages were devoted to a fire in Manchester about a year ago that had burned down a factory belonging to Sir Curry. In the aftermath, the unfortunate entrepreneur went bankrupt and hung himself.

Although it was unclear whether the fires had been caused by an arsonist or by circumstances, in each case the most important British armouries were destroyed. This led to the rise of Bollinger's factory.

"Again we see how naive we were," said Holmes as he read the clippings. "She planned each move well in advance, to the smallest detail, and with extraordinary callousness. She prepared the affair with Bollinger for more than a year. The burning of the Curry factory was her first step on the road to power."

The detective turned the pages.

We learned that her crimes were even more far-reaching and monstrous than we had imagined. The Darringfords' murders and power games were only the tip of the iceberg. In the album, a sort of diary of crime, we uncovered the rotten foundations.

Anyone unfortunate enough to be lured into their web of extortion, bribery or money was eventually eliminated from the game without mercy. They abducted children, murdered, burned houses and factories. In addition to the Curry factory they were responsible for the destruction of at least two other factories in France and one in Italy. This served to increase the influence of the companies that they already controlled. A competitive advantage *par excellence*.

Yes, the suffragettes sometimes lit fires; but Alice's pyromania and profiteering were monstrous. It was only a matter of time before the suffragettes turned their backs on her.

The last pages of the album were devoted to Holmes's funeral.

Here the lady exercised a care approaching fetishism. The clippings were surrounded by childish drawings depicting Holmes' death and were framed with black flowers and decorative ornaments.

The detective cast aside the album. It had ceased to interest him.

We found a few more smoke bombs behind the books, but otherwise there was nothing. When we reunited with the police officers in the hallway, we learned that similar caches of bombs had been prepared throughout the house. Lady Alice had been ready to escape at a moment's notice.

Mycroft told us that his patrol would remain in the villa a while longer and would be joined by professional criminal investigators for a more thorough inspection.

"I would wager that this house still has not revealed all of its secrets," said Holmes.

We made our way to the spacious cellar, which we entered through a door hidden in an alcove behind the stairs. In addition to old bric-a-brac, metal stoves, chests, furniture and similar things, there was nothing unusual or striking, except for the marks in the dust left behind by the retreating lady and her retinue. In the upper half of the sloping rear wall there was an open casement window, through which the lady and her people had disappeared. Streaks of morning light now shone through it.

Mycroft returned upstairs, as he was not inclined to exert himself physically, but Holmes took off his jacket and used an overturned stool to lift himself through the casement to the garden. I followed him, surprised by just how arduous it was. Alice must have been tremendously agile.

We found ourselves on the lawn in front of the garage, near the inconspicuous side gate.

The detective explored the plot thoroughly, but there were not many clues to be found.

"Three pairs of women's shoes, one man's," he said, counting the footprints. "The man's shoeprints are deeper; he appears to have been carrying something heavy. Everything that the lady considered absolutely necessary and that she managed in her haste to collect."

"In particular anything that would reveal where she has escaped to…"

"Precisely. Look, he laid down the duffle bag here; the grass is flattened and the dew has been displaced. The footsteps of course lead to the gate."

The heather-covered gate led out to a dirt road, around the corner from the main access routes. The view of it was blocked by hedges and trees, hence the police officer had not seen them flee.

"A car was waiting for them here," said Holmes, stroking his chin. "No doubt she had it parked here at the ready. The footsteps go no further. According to the tire tracks in the soil it is a common Model T Ford. And the trail is lost on the main road."

Even my friend's genius could no longer follow the trail.

"My man no doubt noticed the car turning from the dirt road," said Mycroft, who had again joined us. "Evidently he did not attach any significance to it. He did not see the lady and assumed the car was just driving past."

"Yes, he assumed," said Holmes, "a common problem among policemen."

"She cleaned up after herself thoroughly," I said, sighing.

"Not as well as she thinks," said Holmes.

He walked across the garden to the main entrance of the villa and its marble staircase. I locked the gate behind us and ran after him and Mycroft. I had my work cut out to catch up to them, they had such long strides.

We rushed into the drawing room where we had first met Alice and where she had received us a few days earlier. The detective went straight to the display of family photographs. He stopped before the photograph depicting the lady with her brother and the Silver Ghost.

"She left the most important thing behind," the detective exclaimed.

"What is that?"

"A map to her hideout!"

He removed the photograph from the frame and pointed to the castle in the background.

"Where else would she escape to? I presume it will not be hard to find."

"I thought that was Darringford!"

"No, Darringford is an old manor house," said Holmes, placing the photograph in his breast pocket. "It does not correspond to the description, location, architectural style or size of this place. Nor is she foolish enough to run home. After all, Scotland is full of potential hideouts."

He looked around once more and then headed back to the garden, where most of the policemen had returned to their work.

The bushes they had pulled up lay in a heap behind the gazebo, above which buzzed angry bees, as though attempting to gather as much pollen as possible before the flowers dried out. At the edge of the beech grove was a mound of earth and the men were taking turns digging and shovelling the soil.

The hole was already quite deep.

"Nothing yet, sir!" the sergeant said to Mycroft.

"Please continue, the body must be there," said the detective's brother.

"How is the work proceeding?" Holmes asked.

"Quite well," answered the sergeant. "The soil is loose and not overgrown with roots."

He was not accustomed to manual labour and was sweating.

"Excellent!" said the detective happily. "That means someone was digging here recently."

He sat down with us in the gazebo. From there we eagerly watched how the dig progressed. The work indeed was going well. With each strike of the shovel we became tenser with excitement.

After a while Holmes could no longer stand idly by. He borrowed a spade from an old corporal and started digging. Presently, whether by luck or fate, his spade hit a solid wooden board.

Those of us sitting in the gazebo could easily distinguish the dull sound.

We ran over and peered into the six-foot pit at the bottom of which Holmes was clearing away the last layer of dark, wet clay with his bare hands. Finally, under the layers of soil, a cracked lid appeared.

Holmes felt for the edge of the board and with the help of one of the officers gave it a mighty yank and threw it aside. Below us lay something wrapped in a canvas. Based on the shape it was not hard to guess what it was.

"A knife!" the detective cried, extending his hand without taking his eyes off his find. His nails were filthy and the tips of his fingers were raw from the digging.

The sergeant handed him a knife. Holmes plunged the blade into the canvas and we heard a ripping sound.

I crossed myself.

There was no doubt that we were standing over the grave of Lord Bollinger, although it was impossible to distinguish any specific features from the remains. They had remained hidden in Lady Darringford's garden for too long and the body had begun to decompose.

The canvas and the dead man's clothes were stuck together, and when the detective pulled them back we could see the worms swarming and feasting on the body. Some of the men immediately turned away from the pit. The rest of us took off our hats.

"His watch," whispered Mycroft hoarsely. "Give me his watch."

The detective obediently slid his hand under the rotting wet jacket and pulled out the dead man's watch chain. His brother leaned over and grasped it in his handkerchief.

"There is no longer any doubt," he said. "The coat of arms belongs to the royal family. Gentlemen, pay your respects to Lord Bollinger."

We straightened up and remained for a moment in silence.

Then my companion climbed out of the ditch and the policemen covered it up. Later that day police investigators arrived at the scene as well as a hearse to pick up the remains.

There were now no more surprises in the opulent villa and its magnificent garden. We returned to my house, from where we would continue the search for Lady Alice. I, however, after the physically and emotionally harrowing experiences of the morning, retired for the remainder of the day.

Holmes too disappeared into his room. Unlike me, however, he did not need to rest his nerves. He simply wanted to remove his disguise.

"It is such a relief to be able to shave," he said to me on the way home. "I am looking forward to being myself again!"

XII
The Adventure Continues

My friend's true resurrection occurred when he finally discarded the beard, the pomade in his hair, the glasses and the Cedric-style clothes. For the first time since his coronary several weeks ago, he stood before me as I and his admirers knew him. With his lightly shaved pointy beard he was now ready to confront any enemy and to pursue the Darringfords as himself. The newspapers printed an official denial of his death in bold letters, and we immediately afterwards received letters, telegrams and cards from well-wishers as well as people with various requests.

Journalists bombarded him with requests for interviews. But the detective had never granted any before and stayed true to his convictions. His time was too precious to devote to prattle and to the disingenuous questions of these riffraff.

Our work again moved from the field to the dusty archives of register offices. The day after Alice magically vanished from her house and Holmes appropriated the photograph of her and her brother standing in front of the stone castle, we launched an investigation in search of this mysterious fortress.

It was painstaking work. It took us two days just to find all the available photographs of Scottish castles and strongholds in the historical institute and royal library, and we spent the next day endlessly comparing them with the castle in the Darringford photograph. I never knew how many castles there were in Scotland! Our work was frustrated by the fact that our photograph of the castle was only from one angle, so we sometimes had no recourse but to refer to our spatial imagination.

"The circle has narrowed to twelve possible locations," said Holmes late in the afternoon of the third day, when we had examined the last of the archival photographs.

"That's quite a lot."

"It is not much when you consider how many we started with," said the detective reading his notes and drumming his fingernails on the desk.

No doubt he wanted to smoke. He was watching me from the corner of his eye to see if I would let him have tobacco, but I did not relent.

I did not hold out much hope that he would listen to my advice for long. But for now the memory of his coronary was fresh in his mind, so he tried to listen to me.

I examined the list.

"Are we going to Scotland then?" I asked. "Shall we go from castle to castle and knock on the door until the lady herself opens? It seems very time consuming."

"That's how the police would go about it," said Holmes. "We will use our brains."

He unfolded a map of Scotland and marked the positions of the castles that corresponded to the photographs. They were separated by hundreds of miles, from Aberdeenshire to Inverclyde, Orkney to West Lothian.

Visiting all of them would require many cold and damp days.

"Is the castle that we are looking for inhabited or abandoned? They are no doubt hatching their plans in secret."

The detective nodded thoughtfully.

"A keen observation, my friend, but unfortunately not to the point," he said. "It could be the headquarters of one of their sympathisers."

"No matter how I look at it, I can't find the key to figuring out which castle is the right one," I admitted. "They are spread out across the entire country and the photograph contains no other point of orientation that would give us a clue."

"Correct," said Holmes. "But let us look at it from the other side. Indeed, the absence of orientation points on the photograph can be just as important."

He again studied the map alongside the photographs of the castles, taking into account the features of the landscape in the background. He measured contours, calculated sizes and distances, factoring in each bit of information to reveal something about the environment.

"We can eliminate two more castles," Holmes said happily, crossing off two points from the map, one on the north coast and the other near Glasgow.

"On what basis?"

"Dunvegan is near Caisteal Maol on the Isle of Sky, it is surrounded by water. The angle from which Darringford's castle is photographed must show the water, but around it there are just plains, so we can exclude Dunvegan."

"And the other?"

"Cathcart Castle. I eliminated it due to its position. It stands on a rocky coastline and in the centre of a rather populous locality, where secrecy would be difficult."

"In that case we ought to focus our efforts on the Scottish highlands."

Of the remaining sites there were five that appeared as though they could be located in these endlessly rolling plains. Nevertheless it was progress. Holmes found a map of the Scottish highlands and spread it on top of the other map.

"Ackergill Tower, Leod, Freswick, Glinney and Dalcross Castle," he said, counting off the remaining castles.

All seemed in play.

"Could the lady have said anything that was a clue?"

His face registered a flash of surprise and his eyebrows rose in astonishment.

"Of course, Watson! I had almost forgotten!"

"What do you mean?"

"Do you remember what Alice said when she parted company with us?"

"Only a tirade of insults."

"And?"

"She expressed regret that the reports of your death were premature."

"The information is staring you in the face, yet you do not see it!" Holmes's mood had clearly improved. He again saw a trail of clues where I saw nothing. This always made him feel mischievous and cheerful. I was glad to be a source of amusement.

"She said that we do not even know who she is and what she plans to do," he said.

"Does it mean anything?"

"It might, but we will not find out here," he said, hitting the desk with his palm and giving the order to leave.

I blindly followed him outside into the street. But when I realised that his brisk steps were taking us straight to the London registry office my heart sank with the thought of rummaging through more musty archives.

"Don't worry, we know exactly what we are looking for this time!" he said.

He asked the archivist for a file about the Darringfords.

"When I was investigating Lady Darringford's past, for some reason I only found information about Bloody Sunday," he explained. "When you reminded me of her comment it occurred to me why I did not get deeper."

The archivist sat us at a desk with a lamp and left us alone with a thick dossier. It contained a genealogical tree of the noble family all the way to its roots. The information that we found in it surprised us!

"It says here that Lord Percy Stanley Hubert Darringford and his wife Margaret had only one son, Rupert!" said the detective with astonishment, searching in vain for a mention of Alice Darringford.

"But that's not possible!"

"But it is, look," he said, handing me the document.

Indeed, Lady Alice did not appear in the official genealogical tree of the family whose name she so proudly bore.

"Where did she come from? Did she deceive everyone?"

"She has been living as Sir Rupert's sister in London for at least two decades," the detective said thoughtfully. "Mycroft confirmed her identity, and we even have a photograph of her with her so-called brother. It is unlikely that she would be just passing herself off as a noblewoman. She needs a solid foundation for her criminal agenda. Certainly she would not risk premature disclosure of her false identity. Lady Darringford she truly is, but how did she become part of the family?"

Sherlock Holmes leaned back in his chair and rested his chin on his fingers.

"She might be the old man's illegitimate offspring?" I said. "A stepdaughter?"

"Doubtful. He would still have to publicly acknowledge her and that would appear here."

"Could she be pretending to be Rupert's sister while in fact being his wife or mistress?"

"Impossible. There would be records of a wedding and my brother would surely know about that. Do not forget that Alice was already Lady Darringford on Bloody Sunday when the police arrested her. The family posted bail for her. She was still too young. No, there must be another explanation."

He again plunged into the papers, determined to discover where and when our femme fatale had emerged. That she had come from the very depths of hell we already had no doubt. But what was the mystery of her origin?

"Here it is!" the detective whooped. "Though she is not bound to Rupert by kinship or blood, in a sense she truly is his sister!"

"Please, Holmes, no more riddles!"

Holmes finished reading the page and shook his head in disbelief.

"Imagine that Alice became part of the family in 1885 at the age of fifteen. The Darringfords took her in as a foster child from the convent in Anges."

"From a convent? She is an orphan?"

"There is nothing here about her real parents," he said, leafing through the pages. "Just that the Darringfords quickly adopted Alice and that she took the family name. In all probability they did not want to risk another pregnancy due to their son's illness. Still, they longed for another child. Alice's real name does not appear in the records; perhaps it was not even kept. And as the old lord and lady died in 1891, there is no one who recalls the events who can help us."

"The death of the foster parents who saved her from the convent must have been a great blow," I said. "Maybe that's what made Alice seek revenge on the world."

"You see good even in the devil," said Holmes, patting me on the shoulder. "But I must disappoint you. The Darringfords died in a barn fire on their estate."

Another fire. I understood what Holmes was trying to tell me. The death of her foster parents was no accident, just like all of those fires in the munitions factories.

"She needed to bury the secret of her origins," said the detective. "Her Machiavellian scheming dates to 1891. She took advantage of her brother's mental illness and over time she poisoned his mind even more!"

"Disgusting," I shuddered. "But how shall we discover her hiding place when she thwarts any attempt to uncover her past?"

"We must once again travel," he declared. "To the convent in Anges!"

**

Scotland, the homeland of my mother. A deep green valley, wedged into the majestic mountains reflected in peat-coloured lakes and wetlands covered with heather. A land of purple-tinted moors and pastures, lush grass and yellow-green cushions of moss, swamps, lilies and blooming flowers. To the east there are beaches and to the west and centre lies a region of uncultivated grassland with a sprinkling of oat fields.

I was glad that we had to go on this journey. Here peace and quiet reigned. We could wander through the countryside the entire day without encountering a soul.

In London one does not have the chance to enjoy nature. In our investigations Holmes and I rarely had the opportunity to venture into the very heart of the wilderness that our country hid. In Scotland one could see deer as big as in a fairytale, eagles soaring high overhead, and fresh wild streams full of salmon and trout. And of course the ubiquitous sheep.

We took the overnight train and the next morning found ourselves in the small town of Anges. Except for the barest necessities we had very little with us in the way of luggage. From the poor, simple train station we headed straight to the inn. It was a typical stone building with a dark thatched roof and an even more typical owner, preserved alive in a brine of thick rye whiskey.

To our query regarding vacancies he replied gruffly that today he had only one room and began rambling about the shabbiness and poverty of the local people. We did not want to become entangled in a long conversation with this bored Scotsman, whose thick Gaelic accent we could barely understand, and so went to our cosy attic room, ate some strong chicken broth, and immediately headed out.

"No matter what they tell us in the convent I can feel in my bones that we are on the right trail," said Holmes, peering at the map.

"How do you know?"

"Anges is directly on the way to Glinney, which is one of our other possible castles."

"Do you think that the lady returned to the place of her youth?"

"Criminals do have a tendency to return to the scene of the crime," he said.

He pointed the way and we embarked on the long walk to the convent.

It was a beautiful day. The sun was pleasantly warm and the blooming meadows gave the normally rough-looking plains a softer aspect. We followed the map up a dirt trail over a hill and up through a pine forest, behind which lay the mysterious place of Alice's origin.

Except instead of the convent we found a ruin.

XIII
Modus Operandi

The term scorched earth was completely apt to describe what we found in the large clearing where the convent should have stood. Extending before us were the weathered ruins of what once used to be a convent, overgrown with ivy and long ago abandoned.

"What happened here?" I stammered.

"They no doubt know at the inn, but I shall hazard a guess," said Holmes, gazing at the ruins.

Upon closer inspection it was immediately clear to us what had destroyed the convent. As we stepped among the dilapidated walls we saw charred stones and blackened beams, now covered in lush vegetation. The floor was completely collapsed, leaving only the bare portion of the perimeter walls. In addition to the central building we made out the outline of side wings and seminaries, now completely overgrown. The farm buildings of the monastery and garden remained buried under the soil. Our voices must have been the first sound in ages to break the pervasive silence.

"I do not want to jump to conclusions, but I fear that I recognise the handiwork of our firebug," said the detective, bending over the grass.

In the sunlight something was shining.

"It is all over now," I said. "The secret of her origin is lost."

"Do not give up hope just yet."

In his hand Holmes held a small cross covered with mould and warped by fire. A forgotten artefact and silent witness to the tragic events. It was symbolic of our quest.

"To what church did the convent belong?" I asked.

"It is hard to determine from what can be seen here," said the detective.

He put the cross in his pocket. As there was nothing else that could be of use to us here, we turned around and headed back to town. Along the way, Holmes discoursed about the local religions, which have had a greater influence here than in other parts of the country.

Talking thus we returned to Anges.

The innkeeper was still loitering around drunkenly and did not require much in the way of encouragement to tell us about the burned down convent.

"You should've asked me, I would've told you that it's pointless to go poking about there," he began, more willing to talk now that my friend had ordered a round of his preferred spirits.

It happened in the winter twenty years ago, when the innkeeper's beloved father, the original owner and founder of the roadside establishment, died. The fire apparently started at night, spreading from the kitchen to the dining room and the adjacent library. By the time the smoke woke up the nuns and they had warned their wards of the danger, the fire had spread so far that nothing could be saved. The few men who lived in the farm buildings and helped run the monastery barely managed to save the girls' lives. There was no time to fight the fire. Despite the porter's efforts, the fire was not without tragic losses. The flames took the lives of three nuns. It was never discovered who started the fire and how.

"You say that the fire originated in the library?" said Holmes.

"Aye," said the man, nodding his round head and spitting tobacco on the floor.

"Are you quite certain?"

"As certain as a man can be after all these years," he said, scratching his head. "I wasn't up there you know. But that's what people said, on my honour!"

"Do you know what this means, Watson?" said the detective, turning to me victoriously. "Once again I am not mistaken! Alice attempted to destroy the convent archive. And she succeeded!"

The talkative innkeeper, happy to have guests who were generous and obviously much more solvent than his usual rural clientele, and delighted to be of service, took no time in imparting some other important information.

"I can see this interests you, gentlemen," he said, leaning over the counter jovially. "Well, if you really need to know the details, then you've got to talk to old lady Donovann who lives over the hill."

"Excellent! We shall go see her right away," said Holmes joyfully, throwing a couple of coins on the counter, indicating his desire to pay and leave.

"Problem is Donovann went to Fadden market and will only get back late at night," said the man, quickly pocketing the coins. "Tomorrow morning I'll show you how to get to her farm."

We were thus condemned to spend the rest of the afternoon in the company of our jovial drunk. We had already had our share of walking, but we were nevertheless happy to learn about the local folklore.

In the evening a few villagers from out of the way settlements came to spend the night at the small inn. They corrected our preconceived notions about Scots, such as their oft-ridiculed greed. In my opinion the Scots are not especially miserly. They simply value money more, because it is so hard to come by.

Indeed the innkeeper and his comrades were most obliging. Holmes invented a heartrending tale about how he was searching for his niece, who he supposed was a ward of Anges convent, and everyone outdid each other with ideas about how to help him. But they all agreed that the best course of action was to see the woman to whom the innkeeper was to take us tomorrow morning.

On the whole it was a pleasant evening with amiable company. The detective contributed a few of his tales of adventure, though not in the first person, but rather as stories he had heard.

He sensed that as Englishmen we were only tolerated here and he did not want our hosts to think we represented the official authorities. We did not forget their national pride. They had never buckled under our rule and were still trying to gain independence. Hence their toughness, brought about by natural conditions and by the constant struggle for survival.

"The Scots are not historically very well represented in British art, music and literature, but their artlessness is so refreshing!" Holmes said to me that night as we nodded off in massive wooden beds under down blankets.

True, we had to accustom ourselves to a certain crudity, but on the other hand the Scots are well known for their technical ingenuity and inventiveness.

I slept peacefully for the first time in many nights, without dreaming of Lady Alice and murderous suffragettes. In the morning I hopped out of bed as lively as a fiddle. Holmes had also slept well and over breakfast he spoke enthusiastically about returning to his farmstead and his bees.

The innkeeper was true to his word and took us to the old woman's farm. A white mist was forming above the green pastures and hillsides.

"Old Mrs Donovann was the superior of the convent," he said to Holmes. "She still lives here. She's almost seventy."

"The church did not relocate her after the fire?"

"No, because she left the order. She stayed here and went into business for herself. She's a resourceful old lady and sometimes girls from town come to help her."

After walking a few miles through a field we were able to make out the retired abbess from a distance. A hunched figure bent over a spade was digging up soil and planting vegetables. Bluish smoke rose from the chimney and all the windows of the house were wide open. In the shed lay a big black dog with white chest and rust-coloured paws. As soon as he saw us he began barking and pulling on the chain.

The old woman straightened up, turned to face us and shielded her eyes. We could not see her face because a scarf was tied around her head.

We doffed our hats and waved. She scolded the dog and went back to work. We kept a good distance from the dog and walked up to her.

"Good morning," said Holmes as we approached.

She continued planting tiny green seedlings without raising her head.

The detective repeated his greeting more loudly.

"It is almost noon," grumbled the old nun.

Indeed the sun was already high in the sky. For peasants and farmers, who woke up long before dawn, it was nearing time for lunch.

"We have been sent from the city to see you," said Holmes.

Still nothing.

He coughed with confusion and wanted to tap the woman on the shoulder, but the dog did not like that. He barked again and tried to pounce on us. Only the strong chain saved us from a mauling. But he pulled the heavy kennel several yards before his strength gave out.

"I say, Mrs Donovann, they have sent us from the city," the detective shouted.

"I'm not deaf," said the woman quietly.

"Excuse me, but I need to talk with you."

"I don't know what I ought to tell you."

"My name is Sherlock Holmes and this is my colleague Dr Watson. We need to ask you a few questions about the convent."

"The convent burned down long ago and I'm no longer a member of the order."

"Nevertheless you are the only one who can answer certain lingering questions."

"Then they will remain unanswered."

It all seemed pointless. The abbess would not deign to talk to us and I feared that if we bothered her a moment longer she would release the barking terror upon us, whose chops were no doubt already salivating. I respected dogs and felt a creeping sense of danger in their presence ever since Holmes and I encountered the terrible fangs of the hound of the Baskervilles. I never quite lost these fears, no matter how hard I tried.

I assumed that the detective would resign himself to defeat, but I was mistaken.

He searched his pocket until he found the cross that he had discovered in the ruins the day before. Just like yesterday it shone as he held it by the chain before the eyes of the stooped nun. She paused, stopped digging in the dirt and straightened.

Then I saw her face and understood why she wore a scarf even on a warm day.

The entire left side of her face was disfigured. From her neck to the border of her grey hair ran a row of tiny scars, almost certainly caused by fire. The purplish skin which once had suffered severe burns had never completely healed. The heat had also burned off the eyebrow over the left eye, which now gaped at us blindly.

She must have been accustomed to the expressions of horror that people had when they looked on her.

She looked at us carefully and took the cross. She gripped it tightly in her bony hand and then returned it to Holmes.

"It was a long time ago," she whispered. "It belongs to another life."

"Keep it," said Holmes, pressing it back into her hand. "Perhaps you have forsaken God, but he has not forsaken you."

The nun's healthy eye flashed and she sank her spade into the ploughed field. She put the cross in the pocket of her long skirt and wiped her mud-caked hands on her apron.

Then she glared at me. "You are a doctor?" she said, coughing.

When I replied in the affirmative the woman motioned us to follow her to the house. But she did not take us inside. We walked past the stone doorway, around the building and into a dank earthen sty, where a goat was resting on a bed of straw. The animal was obviously sick. The goat was listless and judging by the feed that lay untouched in its trough had not been eating. From the corner of the barn the old woman brought a barrel, at the bottom of which was a bit of milk. It was reddish and smelled foul.

"This is what she gave yesterday," said the woman. "Can you help her?"

The goat had a fever and based on the colour of the milk I concluded that there was inflammation of the udder, a relatively frequent disease among goats. Although I am not a specialist, I took some tablets from my medical bag and poured out a few.

"Give her these for a couple of days," I said. "And milk her at least three times a day until the inflammation subsides. Make sure that your hands are clean. And replace her litter; it is important that it is clean and dry."

164

She thanked me. Thus we earned an invitation to tea. The detective was satisfied. Before the kettle on the iron stove had begun to whistle, he gained the coveted answers to his questions.

"We are looking for a girl – indeed now a woman – who spent several years in the convent," he said.

"I knew everyone who passed through those doors. What is her name?"

"Her given name is Alice. We do not know her surname."

"Alice..." she said, running the name on her tongue as though she were examining its taste. Her wrinkled face became contemplative.

"She was born in 1870 or 1871 and in 1885 she left as a ward of the family of Lord Darringford, who later adopted her," said Holmes.

The old abbess gasped.

"I know of whom you speak," she said. "But I cannot tell you anything about her."

"Why not?"

"She was quiet and thoughtful. She avoided others. It was so long ago, I don't even remember how she left for the Darringfords. You would find everything in our records, but..."

She did not finish her sentence and inadvertently pulled the scarf over her face. The old memories had reawakened her pain.

"After the hell fire nothing remained."

"Naturally, I understand," said Holmes. "But I am more interested in the circumstances under which she came to you."

"Yes, of course. It is shrouded in so many strange things that cannot be forgotten."

She paused and poured us some weak tea before continuing with her tale.

"It was at night in the autumn or winter of 1883. I remember it was raining dreadfully. I was roused out of bed by a mighty banging on the door. Behind the door I found Alice. She was twelve years old. She was brought by her father, or at least that's who he introduced himself as. He begged me to take in the child and hide her. He said that he was haunted by a diabolical enemy who would stop at nothing. He was more worried about her than about himself; she was everything to him."

"What was his name?"

"He did not say. He was terrified; I could see the panic in his eyes."

"Can you describe him?"

"He was tall, about your height, with a high forehead, not much hair, and an intelligent face. He was older and well-dressed. And he had very good manners. His daughter too was well brought up."

Holmes listened to the description of the mysterious man with bated breath.

"Cleary he came from a well-situated family. When I took the girl in he immediately disappeared and never appeared again. Neither he nor the girl ever mentioned the mother. For months she cried every night. But they had not forgotten her entirely; they sent her packages and letters. Nevertheless, Alice suffered the whole two years that she spent with us. She was not accustomed to such simple conditions and always wanted to have a candle or lamp next to her. She longed for her father. She was very close to him."

"But he had found a place where his enemy would not find her," said the detective.

"Perhaps. In any case, the Darringfords were a liberation for this poor girl."

A fine liberation indeed, I thought to myself, aware of how she had repaid them.

"That is all I know," said Donovann. "She vanished as suddenly as she had appeared. About six years after her departure the convent burned down."

"This happened in the autumn of 1891?"

"Yes."

"You are certain?"

"The year is branded on my face," she said.

We thanked the old woman for talking to us and got up to leave. She and the dog walked us back to town.

Holmes whistled.

"Watson, I believe that this visit has been most useful! We now finally have Alice's full life story, thanks to which I can now analyse her motives for these horrible crimes."

"How did this shy girl become so vicious?"

"The key is the father," said the detective. "He hid Alice in the convent. The girl was unhappy here and she came to know a world without men."

"Thus her suffragette sympathies?"

"They were no doubt strengthened by the fact that the rival who took her father away from her in childhood was also a man. But this still does not make of her a murderer."

"Then what?"

"During the Bloody Sunday demonstration in 1887 she was merely a zealous feminist; a few years later she would kill. We know her *modus operandi*, which is fire. She befriended it here in Anges, when it lit her lonely nights. In 1891 she burned her adopted parents and set fire to the convent, in order to remove all trace of her origins. It proved successful, and so she continued to use it on her criminal path and in the building of her munitions empire. But in 1891 something must have happened that changed her, something that inflamed her desire for revenge and power."

"What could have shaken her so profoundly?"

"It is elementary my dear Watson," said Holmes. "The death of her father!"

As always he was right. From the psychological point of view it made absolute sense. I wondered how we could determine the identity of her father, but nothing occurred to me.

We returned to the inn, where that evening the last act of our adventure began to be written.

XIV
The Black Hand

In the afternoon following our visit to Donovann, as we sat by the fireplace discussing how to proceed, a surprising number of people began to congregate in the sleepy inn. Until then Anges had been the quietest and sleepiest of places. Holmes could not resist inquiring about the reason for the commotion.

"Today we have a *ceilidh*," the innkeeper explained jovially.

"I suppose you would call it a party," he added, seeing our uncomprehending looks. "Guests will come, musicians will play and there will be dancing and drinking. And I have something special planned for the men, just you wait, gentlemen. You will see something you won't soon forget!"

Indeed we did not.

The pub that night was full to bursting. People pressed together, leaving space only for a dance floor in the middle of the room. The whiskey and beer flowed and there were roars of laughter and boisterous conversation, as the men told their wild stories. Pairs danced on the wooden floor to the rhythm of bagpipes. But Holmes and I plugged our ears.

Most of the men were dressed in tartan and kilts. The detective and I were among the few wearing trousers and we felt rather conspicuous. But the locals accepted us with the same ease and good cheer as they had the day before. As the *ceilidh* continued, they invited us to join them for the evening's main event.

This was in a barn behind the pub and was chiefly for the men. I went there with great curiosity, but was shocked by the bloody carnage that I found.

In the middle of the barn there was a pit about three feet deep and around it a three-foot high fence. Dozens of men crowded around it on the hard-packed dirt floor, watching with excitement a gruesome spectacle by the light of a kerosene lamp below. Those in the back stood on upturned crates, craning their necks in order to see.

In the ditch a furious little terrier of indeterminate colour was surrounded by a teeming multitude of large rats. The dog darted among them, catching them up in his jaws and breaking their necks with a jerky movement of his head. The rats squealed in terror, but gave as good as they got, biting the dog, the bloody wounds making him even more enraged.

The spectators wagered on how many rats the dog would bite and on whether the rats might kill him. Judging by the chanting this particular terrier was the champion of this disgusting spectacle.

"People come here from far and wide," said the innkeeper proudly.

"How barbaric," I said.

A fat bookmaker shoved his way through the crowd to the innkeeper.

"Boss, Lassie made us a bundle," he said, holding up a crumpled wad of banknotes. "What odds should I put on Green Danny?"

"How does he look?"

"Like a bloody mess. But there's no stopping him when he smells blood."

"All right Fibbs," the innkeeper said, rubbing his hands, "place the same bet as last time."

My blood boiled at the sheer callousness of this entertainment. I sought an advocate in Holmes, but I knew that he was not paying any attention to the bloody fight in the pit. He was staring at spectator man who was standing off to one side against the railing.

He was not a Scot and stood out just as much as we did, with his dark complexion perhaps even more. He was well dressed and clean-shaven. His black eyes under their massive eyebrows watched the fighting in the pit with interest. The match was drawing to a close, there were hardly any rats left alive, and the dog's growls were less fierce.

It appeared to be a draw.

The bookmaker counted off the last seconds on his pocket watch. Then he announced the end of the match. Those few who had won their wagers whooped with joy while the angry losers tossed their tickets to the ground.

Many of them returned to the pub while others arrived for the next match. The owner of the terrier lifted the dog out of the pit and put him in a cage, while the bookmaker gathered up the torn bodies of the dead rats with a shovel.

Among those who stayed was the mysterious stranger, who put his winnings in a portmanteau.

I had no idea why he fascinated Holmes so, but before I could ask him the detective turned to the innkeeper. He whispered something to him, but the innkeeper only shook his head.

"I don't know him, it's the first time I've seen him. He took a room late this afternoon. I think he arrived by the last train. You know, we are pretty famous here, all sorts come. I don't try to hide it; it's legal and popular hereabouts."

"And is rather profitable," said the detective coldly.

"And what of it?" said the innkeeper. "We are not as high and mighty as you gents from London. Nobody would come here for bridge and hot water."

Holmes turned his back to him before anyone could notice their little exchange of opinions, and he pulled me aside to a bale of straw. Meanwhile another dog had been put in the ditch and wagers were being placed. The stench of urine and tobacco mixed with the smell of blood.

"Do you see that man?" said the detective pointing at the stranger.

"Yes, I noticed you eyeing him. Do you think he is important?"

"Perhaps. I suspect that he is Colonel Tankosić."

"Who is that?"

"Do you not read the papers? Vojislav Tankosić!"

"I do not recall ever reading about him. What's it all about?"

"The colonel is one of the most important Serbian nationalists," Holmes explained. "He is a member of the Young Bosnia party, made up of Serbs, Croats and Bosnian Muslims who seek the independence of Bosnia and the unification of all of its occupied territories. Tankosić and others recently founded an even more radical organisation called the Black Hand. The atmosphere in the Balkans is tense; they are preparing for war. The members of the movement are even voluntarily enlisting in the Serbian army. Tankosić leads a Serbian irregular militia that is fighting the Turks in Macedonia."[22]

"But what is he doing here?"

"I am afraid that he too is headed to Glinney. Anges is a necessary transfer point."

"You think he is on his way to a meeting with Alice?"

"Precisely. The consequences of such an alliance could be far-reaching."

"How can a Serbian activist threaten England?"

The detective wiped his sweaty brow.

"The whole world is now a boiling cauldron; you know this all too well yourself. One small spark and everything will explode. You heard what Mycroft said, and Alice is playing her hand. She has already obtained control over the factories. She knows our strategic plans and can blackmail the government, or she can sell secrets to our enemies. If war erupts, her position will only strengthen, as attention will be directed elsewhere. And it will gain her considerable profit. If she supports the Black Hand they will certainly cause the explosion that she needs and her dream of war will come true. The Black Hand will

---

[22] Tankosić was a member of the Central Committee of the Black Hand (Црна Рука), a secret organisation officially called Unity or Death. It was founded in 1911 by Serbian nationalists and participated in the assassination of the heir to the throne Archduke Franz Ferdinand in Sarajevo on June 28, 1914 by activist Gavrilo Princip. Princip had wanted to join the Mladá Bosna movement, but was rejected due to his small stature. He therefore went to Prokuplje to request a personal interview with Tankosić, who rejected him because he was too weak. It is possible that this refusal was one of the reasons why Princip later tried to compensate for his lack of physical strength by committing an exceptional act. The assassination compelled Austria-Hungary to take action against Serbia, which led to the First World War, just as Holmes feared back in 1911.

achieve its political objectives and Lady Darringford will satisfy her lust for power and money."

A sad prophecy. There would never be peace in the Balkans, which was exactly what our lady wanted.

"She spared no time in arranging to negotiate with the Black Hand," I said.

"It was her only play. Now that she knows about us, time is of the essence."

"What shall we do?"

"First we must confirm whether it is in fact Tankosić."

"Will you introduce yourself?"

"I will do it another way. Wait here, I will be back directly!"

So saying he entered into the crowd. The next match was already well underway. The peasants and the stranger were in a kind of frenzy and rhythmically chanted the name Green Danny, a pit-bull terrier who was just now acquainting the rats with his fangs.

Blood spurted from the ruptured arteries and each geyser led to much cheering, applause and stamping. From the back row I watched as Holmes slipped through the crowd to the side of the mysterious man. At the railing the detective leaned as far forward as he could and began waving to encourage the animal combatants. The men behind him did not appreciate this and it led to much shoving and jostling.

I assumed this was the detective's intention. He immediately apologised and pressed himself against the stranger in order to give the unhappy lot behind him a better view. Then I lost track of him as the roaring crowd closed in. I could only guess what was going on in the ring.

174

The mass of bodies blocked my view as the spectators pressed forward as close as possible. It served the detective's ends perfectly. Some twenty minutes later he came back without anyone having noticed anything amiss.

"It is indeed him," he said. "I managed to search him in the confusion. He is not carrying identification papers, unfortunately, but I found a ticket in his pocket for tomorrow's morning train to Glinney. It must be him. As soon as Tankosić comes to an agreement with the Darringfords they will reveal Lord Bollinger's strategic plans and will equip him with those monstrous weapons whose patents they stole. War will be inevitable."

"He must be stopped immediately! He must not get to Glinney."

"No, that will not help us," said the detective. "He is no doubt expected at the castle, and if he does not appear, Alice's suspicions will be raised and she shall again disappear."

"But what else can we do?"

"You are right about one thing, we must act immediately. Midnight is coming. If we set off for Glinney now, we will get there before daybreak."

"You want to travel there by night?" I said horrified.

"There is no alternative. It is our last chance to catch her!"

"It is all too fast!" I croaked. "How will we get there? We don't have any means of transport. And assuming that we do make it all the way to Glinney, what do you want to do when we arrive? We have no way to conquer their fortress and we will never rouse the police so early."

"If you permit, I will address these questions on the way," he said, hurrying out of the barn.

We returned to our room and changed. Holmes grabbed a bag and threw in the most important items that we would need. On the table he left the innkeeper money and a letter in which he asked him to inform certain people should we not return by noon and to send the rest of the luggage to Mrs Hudson in Fulworth.

Only then did he start to arrange transport.

There were only a limited number of methods to choose from. In front of the house stood a parked car and in the stable there were several horses. He chose the latter, even though the car was much faster. They did not belong to us, of course, but Holmes decided that we were entitled to steal them for the higher good.

"If at all possible we will return everything," he said, for good measure scrawling a note with his address onto the boards of the stable.

"Although nobody would hear us start the car, we would never get near the castle in it," he continued. "In the stillness of the night the sound of the engine would alert them to our presence miles away."

He threw a couple of saddles over two burly geldings, tightened the belts, threw the bridle and led them out of the stable before anyone noticed the theft.

I shared his desire to disappear as quickly as possible, for I knew what they did to horse thieves out in the country. I did not relish the thought of being lynched or tarred and feathered.

After helping the detective into the saddle and getting to grips with my horse I was already as battered as a bale of barley.

We did not go fast, but judging by how I bounced and jostled in the saddle it was fast enough.

We had soon left Anges behind us and were headed over the dark hills and plains. It was not the most comfortable mode of travel.

The roads were miserable, the air cold, our clothing insufficient. We were warmed only by the thought, or rather the hope, that everything would soon end one way or another, and we were pushed forward by the terror of the feared Black Hand, the right hand of the devil.

In describing our journey, I will confine myself to saying that for all its beauty and diversity Scotland can be equally austere and inaccessible, especially when darkness falls and submerges the country into fog so thick that you could cut it with a knife. We rode as fast as our horses would go, resting only briefly, covering mile after mile.

Thanks to this punishing ride we indeed arrived in Glinney before sunrise, just as Holmes had predicted. We rode around the town and climbed into the highlands above.

The lofty stronghold emerged before us through the haze.

My heart leapt as I recognised the castle in the photograph. The hideaway in which she had found a refuge for the last phase of her criminal plan.

She had chosen well.

It was a mighty, impregnable mass of stone, surrounded by steep walls. Behind them was a rectangular main building, and two floors of narrow windows and square towers at the sides. We could not see more, but assumed that there were two courtyards behind the large entrance gate to which the path led upwards.

We reined in our horses and stopped. Although we were still a few miles from our goal, we had to proceed the rest of the way on foot. I was short of breath.

"We shall leave the horses here," said Holmes. "There is nowhere to hide them at the castle."

Despite the long ride he dismounted nimbly. Where did he get the energy?

He untied the bag from the saddle horn and tethered the horses to a stake at the side of the road.

"Leave whatever you can. We need to move quickly!"

Easy for him to say; he must have had some perpetual motion machine inside his body, but I was already tired and weak.

But I could not let him go alone. I threw off my warm jacket, leaving just my waistcoat and scarf, and huffed and puffed after him.

We halted under the ramparts and turned away from the main gates, which were locked with several latches. The walls towered above us, but apparently presented no obstacle for Holmes. He examined them carefully, took the bag from his back and pulled out a crossbow with a long rope fastened to the end.

"With a little ingenuity you do not need heavy machinery to conquer the thickest walls. Can you climb with me?" he asked.

"Certainly not!" I gasped.

The detective looked around.

"About thirty yards to your right there is a little door, probably a side entrance," he said pointing. "Go there; I will come for you. If you hear a suspicious noise, run."

Although these days I was not much for running either, I agreed, not wanting to spoil his enjoyment of the plan. I made my way to the spot he had indicated and watched his performance. Taking into account his age and recent health problems, I could only marvel.

He tucked the legs of his trousers into his thick socks and armed the crossbow. He took aim and squeezed the trigger. The anchor with the rope trailing behind it sailed over the massive stone wall and I heard a faint clink as it hit the rampart. Holmes pulled the end of the rope until he was certain it held firm and secured it so that he could start climbing. The knots on the rope supported his hands and feet, as did small chinks in the masonry.

Holmes mobilised all of his strength. He could not give up, not when we had come this far. He pulled himself up the rope methodically, hand over hand, his feet searching for chinks in the masonry, higher and higher up the grey stone wall. No doubt he was cold; he wore only a sweater, and in the dark I saw the white puffs of steam as he exhaled.

Then he disappeared from view and I was alone in the darkness beneath the castle. I buried my hands deep in my pockets and waited crouched at the door. It was about twenty minutes before I heard Holmes quietly steal on the other side of the door and it opened. Over the hill the sun was just rising.

Inside the gate rattled and I slipped inside.

I found myself panting beside the detective in a cold narrow corridor.

He pulled me behind him into the castle, where perhaps only the builder knew the way. The corridors crisscrossed, every now and then unexpectedly dodging to one side, held together by passageways, storage rooms and stairs.

It was dark. Electricity had still not been installed. Sometimes we came across an unlit torch and in the third room Holmes found a kerosene lamp.

"I coiled the rope and hid it on the wall," he said to me, when I finally saw him in the light of the lamp. "I got into the north courtyard. Wait until you see what I found there! Now we must go up to the living quarters. The crucial thing is to retrieve the stolen plans and patents. With a little luck we will get out before they awaken. Then Mycroft will call the cavalry!"

I nodded my agreement.

We scurried from the cellar to a large hall and from there to the grand staircase. The interior of the castle was imposingly vast, but simple, and was silent except for the distant tinkle of cups in the kitchen. The servants were already busy and it was only a matter of minutes before the masters awoke.

We were looking for a study. Surely that was where the Darringfords kept the stolen documents and perfected their schemes.

The windows were very small and all the doors were made of wood, giving the castle a bare character. Here and there was a tapestry, curtains or a dingy suit of armour.

Finally we found it. The door to the study was bolted, but this presented no obstacle for Holmes, who expertly picked the lock.

We went in, leaving the door open just a crack behind us so that we could hear if someone was coming down the corridor.

The centre of the room was dominated by a massive round desk. It was covered with plans, maps, patents, samples of secret chemicals, and letters, which Alice and her brother studied late into the night. Apparently they felt so secure here that they did not even bother to put them away for the night or lock them in a safe. Next to them on the desk were a couple of plates and two unfinished glasses of red wine.

The detective eagerly gathered up the documents and hurriedly examined them.

"Patents from Minutti's factory, copies of the originals that Pascuale showed us," he cried. "I would not be surprised if his office is soon destroyed by a fire. And here are materials from Picard's munitions factory!"

Indeed we found everything, including Lord Bollinger's strategic war plans. Holmes handed me the most important documents and I stuffed them under my waistcoat. I had no other way to carry them.

"Please take a look around," he asked me, fully employed with the jumble on the table. There was still a large wardrobe and chest in the corner that needed to be searched.

I looked through the chest, but did not find anything noteworthy.

"Interesting," my friend suddenly mumbled. He stopped rummaging through the papers on the desk.

"What?"

"There are several documents here that confirm what I had suspected."

He handed me a few of them.

The first was a letter from Emmeline Pankhurst, an official representative of the suffragette movement, expressing strong reservations about some of Alice's actions. Although nothing of what the lady did had been made public and or performed openly on behalf of the secret faction, Mrs Pankhurst must have suspected something.

And she did not like it.

In the missive she distanced herself and the movement from Lady Darringford and warned her not to seek her ends under the auspices of the movement. The letter was dated several days ago.

It appeared to be the end of a long friendship.

"It seems that Alice and her brother's plans are beginning to crumble," I said.

"For the time being it is not critical. They have obtained what they needed, and as soon as the suffragettes realise the power that Alice has gained they will no doubt accept her once again."

The second document was much more alarming.

It was something in German. From the little that I still remembered of the language, I understood that it was an order for military hardware.

So here too the Lady was negotiating the sale of British strategic plans with a no doubt highly placed German official.

The wheels of the war machine had begun to turn. We had come at the eleventh hour.

I added the documents to the others under my waistcoat and Holmes handed me a few more. I was already stuffed like a pillow, but in the wardrobe I fortunately found a travel tube with a carrying strap. I rolled up everything that I could into it and slung it over my shoulder.

Besides the tube the spacious and deep wardrobe contained nothing but coats and shoes.

I wanted to close it, but as I turned towards Holmes, I noticed in the mirror on the opposite wall the door opening and somebody entering.

My heart almost stopped beating, but I could not warn the detective without drawing attention to myself. I took a few steps back, ducked inside the wardrobe and closed the door behind me. The detective raised his head and immediately understood what was happening.

He did not panic. He calmly turned to face the entrance to the room and stood still. In the crack between the doors I could watch what unfolded.

Lady Darringford entered brandishing a small pistol. Despite her perverse nature, she still looked like the most beautiful woman in the world.

"I was expecting your visit," she said. "Nevertheless you are here early."

"Better too early than too late."

"It is too late for you anyway and for the rotten world as we know it."

"What has made you despise the world?" said Holmes, shaking his head sadly.

"Men, Mr Holmes! Two representatives of this sordid species in particular."

"Men? Why this hatred? Indeed, I thought that a man, your father, was your role model."

"Do not dare utter his name in your filthy mouth!" she cried. "My father was the last real man and you are not even close to his equal! You were just lucky!"

"No doubt," he agreed.

"John Clay was the first to take my father away from me," she continued. "I assume there is no need to introduce him to you."

"Of course not," he said. His eyes suddenly widened with discovery. He already knew what my mind was still searching for.

"Do you want to hear who the second fiend was who took my father from me for good?" said the lady, her face so close to Holmes's that their noses almost touched.

The detective bowed his head.

"No, I know who it was," he said sadly. "It was me."

Holmes? For God's sake, how was he responsible for Alice's madness? There was only one possibility. But it was so unthinkable that I could hardly believe it.

XV
A Dish Best Served Cold

Revenge is a dish best served cold and few things today were colder than Professor Moriarty's remains beneath the Reichenbach Falls.[23]

But his daughter had made it clear to us. Oh Alice, why must you be that devil's daughter?

That it was Moriarty who had hidden his daughter in the convent in Anges was the only possible solution to the riddle that Holmes and I had been trying for weeks to solve.

Her real name was Alice Moriarty.

It shed new light on Lady Darringford's motives. It was about more than just power, money and the desire to mould the course of history. It was about revenge! Revenge against Holmes, who had dispatched her father from the world, and revenge against the world for not understanding and valuing his criminal genius.

The war that Alice and her foster brother had set in motion could bring her everything she desired: A new world order and the realisation of her father's dreams, but on an even larger scale! He had been content with ruling the London underworld. His daughter wanted nothing less than to rule Europe.

---

[23] Sherlock Holmes fought his greatest enemy, the criminal genius Professor Moriarty, to the death on May 4, 1891 at the Reichenbach Falls in Bern, Switzerland. Moriarty did not survive the fall into the depths below, but Sherlock Holmes did. Nevertheless, the detective remained in hiding for several years and only returned to London in the spring of 1894.

She had gravitated towards the suffragette movement, but her militancy was deplorable. It was not the monastery that awakened her opposition towards men; her hatred was self-inflicted. The first wave was caused by John Clay, the uncrowned king of the London underworld in the mid-1880s. We had encountered him as Vincent Spaulding in our investigation of the case of the Red-Headed League.

The nun had described Moriarty in 1883 as a frightened man afraid for his daughter's life. It was hard to imagine the calculating Napoleon of crime in such circumstances. We knew him in a completely different guise. Parental love had apparently overpowered him and we could only guess why events had unfolded as they had. In those days Moriarty already had grand criminal ambitions, but Clay controlled the breeding grounds of all London. Their power struggle was fierce, so the professor had to get rid of his Achilles heel.

In order to destroy his rival, Moriarty put his daughter somewhere where Clay could never find her.

In 1890 the royal hand of justice fell on Clay's shoulder. But this was just the last in a series of reversals. Moriarty had risen to the pinnacle of power, but this did not help Alice, who still could not return to her father's arms. Clay had disappeared, but an even more formidable adversary had appeared: Sherlock Holmes. He aimed to destroy the professor's criminal network. Moriarty's daughter would again be an obstacle, so she needed to remain on the sidelines, which by then was with the Darringfords. Difficult months followed for everyone. And before that fateful May 4, 1891 Alice never saw her father again.

Two men had taken her father away from her. Now the whole world had to suffer for it.

First came the murder of the Darringfords, who knew her origin. Then the burning of the monastery. And the fire began to spread further. How madly insane!

Now she stood in the study of her hideaway near the Scottish town of Anges, where it had all begun long ago, pointing a pistol at my companion's chest. I was trembling in my hiding place in the wardrobe, watching through the crack of the door and clutching the stolen documents. They had to be rescued at all costs.

Keeping the pistol aimed at the detective, Alice carefully walked around him and examined the desk. She immediately realised that most of the important documents were gone.

"Where are the papers?" she sputtered.

The detective did not answer and stared at her defiantly. Alice rummaged through the desk, but all she found was a map of Britain.

She took a few steps towards the door and called into the corridor.

"I ask you again, where did you hide them?"

"Ask as many times as you want, I will not tell you."

"Tough talk. But we will see how strong your will is."

A tall man stepped into the study. The sharp facial features were a bit effeminate, but his tight leather pants and loose frilled shirt outlined the broad shoulders and strong muscles. It was probably Alice's servant, whose footprints we had found on the front lawn of her villa.

"Search him!" the lady ordered, still pointing the pistol at the detective.

The man nodded and frisked Holmes deftly. But he found nothing.

187

"He's clean," he said in a high-pitched voice, strangely at odds with the massive physique.

"So where are they?" the lady cried impatiently. "They must be here somewhere!"

"Do you think?" said the detective.

Alice faltered. But not for long.

"Of course, I almost forgot your faithful henchman Watson. He must have them. He cannot have gotten far!"

The effete muscleman searched the room while she impatiently kept Holmes at bay with the pistol. The longer the search lasted and the longer the secret documents remained out of her control, the more nervous she became. Without them her plan was doomed.

When the servant got to the wardrobe I thought I was certain to be discovered. There was no hope. I instinctively pressed myself into the furthest corner, wrapped myself in the coats and stuck my legs into a pair of wellingtons.

But fortune was on my side.

The muscleman quickly frisked the coats, his hand missing my face by an inch. But he did not see me. Thinking that the wardrobe was empty he again closed the doors.

I returned to my vantage place.

Alice was biting her lower lip and looking at my companion with irritation.

"The doctor and all of the documents are already gone," he lied. "Soon the authorities will be here to do their work. Give yourself up while there is still time."

Moriarty's daughter lipped her lips, on which a drop of blood had appeared, and shook her head.

"Perhaps, but something does not sit right," she said quietly. "Why would you stay behind? The doctor does nothing without you."

The detective again fell silent.

"Very well, we will play your game," she said. "William, take the horse and search around the castle for footprints. Follow them, and when you find the good doctor, kill him. Do not return without my documents! And hurry. I meet Tankosić in the afternoon."

The servant left while I lamented at the ease with which the beautiful Alice condemned me to death. I promised myself that if we ever got out of there alive I would never again succumb to the temptations of the flesh.

"I still do not believe you, Holmes," she continued. "I think that in the end you will talk and tell me where our little doctor is hiding."

"You are a fool."

"We shall see," she said. With the pistol pointed at him she led him to the door.

They left the study and disappeared from my sight.

I wondered what to do. I was safe enough in the wardrobe, but to what end? I could die here of hunger without helping Holmes or saving the royal documents.

But leaving the hiding place could mean certain death.

No, I could not just stay there waiting. I had to do something!

I lingered for a few minutes until I was sure that Alice and Holmes were already far enough away. Then I carefully opened the door. The room was empty and the doors to the corridor were wide open.

I checked to make sure I had all the documents and left the room.

There were voices coming from the ground floor.

Creeping on tiptoe I silently made my way to the staircase.

From behind the stone portico I peered through the corridor and into the dining room. At a long table Rupert Darringford was being served breakfast by the woman we had seen in Pascuale's office, the murderess of the factory owner Minutti and the Italian secret service agent Paolo.

Although I was hardly in a position to take advantage of the situation, we finally had the whole little family together.

Lord Rupert had already "welcomed" the detective. Holmes sat at Rupert's right and the whole side of his face was red. Alice sat at the other end of the table. Her brother's interrogation methods evidently greatly amused her.

But no one had ever succeeded in extracting anything from Holmes by force.

"Where is Dr Watson?! Where are my papers?!" Darringford yelled at the motionless detective, wiping his forehead with a napkin, the vein on his temple swollen thick as a finger. Judging by his behaviour our recent diagnosis of him was correct. He clearly suffered from manic psychosis, and his parents had done well not to have another child. Their choice of ward was more disputable.

Lord Rupert soon lost what little patience he had and realised that, try as he might, beating my companion would not get him anywhere.

"We shall do it another way, then" he snorted, tossing aside the napkin. "Let us play a game you and I."

Saying thus he hurried off somewhere.

The detective took advantage of his momentary absence for a last attempt at some sort of negotiation.

"Alice, it is still not too late," he said. "Your father was my great rival and I dare say that he died as such. Our fight was dignified and worthy of its name."

"Save your words, Holmes."

"You will unleash a war in which millions will die."

"Yes, millions! The more the better!" she cried. "After all it will be the men who die. Then women will rule!"

"You mean *you* shall rule. Even the suffragettes know this and have disowned you!"

"They still do not understand!" she fumed. "I offered them the world and they dithered and trembled. All I wanted was their tacit support. At least the wheat has been separated from the chaff. My faithful core has remained!"

"Faithful? Do you mean Pastor Barlow?"

"Barlow? Please!" she laughed. "He served his purpose and then he had to go. He is now stuffing his face somewhere else, whether with ambrosia in heaven or with cockroaches in hell. No, by the faithful I mean the true warriors, not those fools."

Her lady servant, whose shoulders I could see from my vantage point at the top of the stairs, nodded eagerly.

"Those fools probably have other plans," said the detective. "Ones in which blood will not flow."

"Weaklings!"

I was still crouching above the staircase and had no plan but to run into the dining room, cause a panic, grab Holmes and run away. Of course, the chances of its succeeding were practically nil.

Darringford returned to the dining room, brandishing a large revolver.

"Do you know what this is?" he said, sticking it under the detective's nose.

"It is the gun manufactured according to Vito Minutti's patent. The revolver with the shrapnel projectile that killed him."

"Oh, you are not mistaken, my friend," said Rupert, mocking the detective's dignified and even-tempered voice. "But there's one small difference. The one that Veronica used to kill Minutti was just a prototype. This little fellow will turn you into mincemeat!"

"I see. What game shall we play with it?"

"I would also like to know," Alice interjected.

Rupert emptied the cylinder, and the bullets rattled onto the table. He left only one bullet inside. Then he spun the cylinder and the lock clicked.

"It was taught to me by a prince in Moscow," he said laughing. "It is called Russian roulette."

"Rupert, it's too dangerous!" Alice cried.

"Depends for whom," said the Lord. He spat and pointed the barrel at the detective's head.

"You may begin," said Holmes.

"With pleasure!"

Rupert snorted, pointed the gun at the detective, switched off the safety and pulled the trigger. The hammer struck empty. Holmes looked straight ahead without blinking.

Darringford straightened and pursed his lips. His big bushy moustache quivered with excitement.

Holmes looked at him defiantly and raised his eyebrows. Darringford had no choice but to play the game he had foolishly suggested. He pointed the gun to his head, closed his eyes and pulled the trigger firmly.

Once again the chamber was empty.

The Lord, his sister and Veronica all exhaled audibly. It was now Holmes's turn.

Rupert thrust the barrel against the detective's ear and fired. I could not watch. A few seconds of silence in which you could hear a pin drop, and then again an empty click.

There now were only three bullets left. The likelihood that the next one would be deadly was growing.

Holmes must have had nerves of steel. He was still motionless, his tension evident only in his damp brow.

The nobleman meanwhile was drenched in sweat. His hands shook and he brought the revolver to his head reluctantly.

"Rupert," the lady whispered, "I think you should stop playing."

"But I like this game," said the detective wryly. "It is exciting, fair, and impossible to cheat. It is decided by fate and luck."

Perhaps he should have kept his mouth shut.

"Well if you like it so much you can take another round," Rupert cried, removing the revolver from his head and again pointing it at the detective. "We will see what your luck is like!"

"But it is not fair!"

"The world is not fair," said Rupert.

"Shoot!" cried Alice.

He fired.

The deadly bullet remained in the cylinder. There were only two shots left.

Holmes grew pale. I feared for his heart.

"You are a coward who does not even play by his own rules," said Holmes.

Rupert stood as though turned to stone, firmly gripping the handle of the revolver. He had no choice. If he did not want to lose face he had to play the next round.

The odds were not favourable.

But he was saved by his stepsister, who abruptly ended the game.

"Enough foolishness!" she cried, ripping the gun from his hand and throwing it on the floor. It clattered on the stone floor and slid to the door to the corridor. "This will not get us anywhere. We need to find out where that old fool has run off to and retrieve our documents, not get ourselves killed!"

My eyes were fixed on the discarded revolver.

"You are right as always," said Rupert, exhaling.

"Leave everything to me," said Alice, caressing his face as though he were a little boy. "Your sister will take care of it, you just relax."

She controlled him like a puppet. Rupert looked uncertain, but then nodded his head obediently and shuffled to his chair, where he began biting his fingernails.

"You have stolen something from me that I need, Mr Holmes," said the lady. "I shall have to break your fingers."

She walked off and returned with a heavy hammer.

"No! I hate violence," Rupert cried.

Among other things his mind obviously struggled with schizophrenia.

"Turn around then," said the lady.

She faced Holmes and looked at him apologetically.

"Forgive me, his degenerated blue blood is to blame. Sometimes he does not know what he is saying."

She grabbed the detective's left hand, pried apart one of his fingers, and placed it on the table. With one hand she kept it motionless while with the other she swiftly brought down the hammer.

There was a crunching noise and blood spurted.

Though his spirit was unbreakable my companion could not bear the pain. He cried out.

"Has your tongue finally loosened?" said Alice.

"Never!" he cried.

I could not let her torture him any further. While Alice bent over him and chose another finger I leapt from my hiding place, bounded down the steps, and ran for the revolver. Before they could notice me I was standing between the doors to the dining room, aiming the weapon in front of me.

They froze.

Lady Alice straightened and blinked with surprise.

"Well well," she said. "Dr Watson"

"Lay down your weapon!" I ordered. "Nice and easy, slide it towards me!"

She reached inside the pocket of her skirt and removed the pistol. She slid it along the floor, but not towards me as I had ordered, but somewhere behind her, where it ended up behind a wardrobe.

Holmes, whose injured hand was bleeding, looked at me with troubled eyes. He must have been in a lot of pain, but it had not broken him.

"You should have run away," he wheezed.

"He's right," said the lady. "Clearly you have not taken into account the laws of mathematics."

I knew what she meant.

There were three adversaries before me. And the revolver contained only one bullet.

XVI
Professor Moriarty's Legacy

In those few seconds I aged a few years.

As I stood in the entrance to the dining room, pointing the revolver at the Darringfords and their murderous assistant, I realised that my desire to save Holmes from the clutches of our enemies had prevailed over common sense. My rash conduct was of little help to the detective. Indeed, I had put myself in danger and risked returning the documents which we had obtained so laboriously.

Then the suffragette Veronica resolved my dilemma of which of the three targets to take aim at first.

She ripped open the hem of her skirt and leapt with a terrible roar onto the fully laid table. She kicked aside the decorative placemats and ran across the table.

Her outstretched hands with their sharp fingernails and her bared saliva-coated teeth were rapidly approaching me.

I later often wondered about and regretted my actions, but at that moment my fingers responded instinctively.

Veronica was moments from hurling herself at me.

But the second-to-last chamber in the revolver was the deadly one.

It went off in my hands and the shrapnel projectile left the barrel with a loud roar. It hit Veronica in the face. The bullet immediately shattered and made her already ugly face even uglier. In short, it ceased to exist. It turned into mincemeat, just as Rupert had said.

Her body hit the floor with a thud, followed by shreds of skin and flesh. One of the dead woman's size five shoes, which in Venice had put us on her trail, flew off and landed near Holmes's chair. Alice's brother laughed madly, but did not move. I opened my mouth and lowered the weapon.

Alice's hand fell limp and the hammer dropped to the floor. Holmes alertly kicked it out of her reach. The noise brought her back to her senses and forced her to act. She shuddered and pushing past the seated detective crossed the dead body of her servant with disgust and jumped right in front of me. I was too surprised by what I had done to be able to resist, but fortunately she did not want to fight.

She shoved me contemptuously and wrestled away the tube containing the documents.

"Who is this scarecrow we have here?" she laughed.

I was powerless to stop her. She took the precious tube from me as though I were a small child. Then she took the documents that were under my waistcoat. She hissed something and ran away.

"Stop her! She must not get away!" cried Holmes attempting to rise from the chair. He clutched his paralysed hand to his body and stumbled after her.

"Rupert, take care of them!" Alice cried, while she feverishly searched for the pistol behind the wardrobe.

Rupert leapt out of his chair, growled like a wild animal, and blocked our path. He turned up the sleeves of his shirt, clenched his fists and assumed a boxer's stance.

My friend and I formed a phalanx around him, hoping that our numerical superiority could overcome his massive fists.

But this was not the case.

Though we hurled ourselves at him it was like two bugs going after an elephant. While I jabbed weakly at his face and dodged his mighty swings, Holmes jumped on him from behind and tried with his good hand to lock him in a half nelson. As this made him a greater danger to Rupert than my pitiful thrusts, the lord diverted his attention from me and turned to the detective.

Alice had meanwhile located the gun, but she did not dare fire while we were wrestling with her brother. Instead she ran off with the documents and disappeared among the columns in the hallway.

Our struggle continued with undiminished intensity. There was a lot at stake. Rupert reached for Holmes with his great paw and flung him lightly over his head.

The detective flew forward and fell between me and the nobleman, stomach first on the ground. He tried to break his fall, but landed heavily on his crushed finger. He groaned and almost fainted from the pain.

Rupert bent towards him, flipped him over on his back and grabbed him by his sweater like a rag doll. He tossed him in the air and flung him onto the table. The breakfast dishes came crashing to the floor as the detective slid across the whole length of the table to the other side, where his body collided with the wall and fell again on the floor.

He no longer even groaned. I was worried that he did not get up.

His lordship roared like an animal and slowly turned towards me. I backed away from him gingerly, but to no avail. This blue-blooded mountain of man lurched at me horribly like a wild buffalo. I stumbled on Veronica's corpse, rolled back and fell in a puddle of blood. I wanted to regain my footing, but my hands and feet slid in the darkening sticky fluid.

What could a man entering the autumn of life do against a hulk of forty in his prime?

But the Lord works in mysterious ways.

I felt like a beetle lying on its back, powerlessly waving its legs while a predator descends upon it. But behind the predator there appeared a shadow with the profile of an eagle.

It was Holmes!

Despite a severe contusion in his hand he was clutching a knight's shield which he had removed from the wall. I would have selected the axe, but the detective never wanted to kill his opponents, just deliver justice.

Darringford was in such a frenzy that he did not notice him.

The detective grimaced as he raised the shield over his head and brought it down on Rupert's bull neck.

For a moment he stood motionless, as though thinking about what had just happened. Then eyes bulging, he staggered and began to fall. He almost fell right on top of me, but Holmes shoved him so that he toppled to the side.

"That was close," I said.

He tossed aside the shield and helped me get up. My shirt was covered in Veronica's blood and stuck to my body. Holmes rubbed his crippled hand and wiped the blood. I took a look at it. The tip of the index finger was crushed and the rest of the fingers were badly bruised.

"By attempting to save me you have proved your friendship," he said. "At the same time you have jeopardised everything that we have worked for!"

"Forgive me," I said.

There was nothing more I could say.

"Do not apologise. We must act. She cannot have gotten far!"

We headed for the hall where we had last seen Alice. From there the doors leading to the courtyard in front of the castle were wide open.

It was already light outside. The sky was filled with clouds and it looked like it would rain.

The yard was full of Moriarty's legacy: heavy machinery produced by the leading munitions factories of Europe, prototypes of weapons for which the owners had paid with their lives. Under wooden scaffolding stood a tank and to the side was a yellow two-seater triplane armed with machine guns. There were also cannons, howitzers and guns of every size and type imaginable, war machines that could plunge the world into catastrophe. These prototypes were waiting here for Tankosić, displayed in all their monstrous glory.

I remembered what Holmes had told me when he collected me at the break of dawn at the side door of the castle. He had been absolutely right.

To the left of where we stood were several low outbuildings.

On our right was a castle gate, enclosed from within by a lattice. When we ran out into the courtyard the gate screeched as it lifted.

There were gunshots. Two bullets dug into the trampled grass in front of us.

Alice's old Model-T Ford burst out from among the vehicles parked at the gate, which included Rupert's Silver Ghost under a canvas. Holmes and I jumped to either side.

While I hid behind the open doors of the castle the detective ran towards the outbuildings.

"We don't have a weapon!" he shouted at me. "Watson, you must find one!"

From where he was he had no chance of finding anything to counter her pistol. Once again I was our only hope. I waited until Holmes reached a position of relative safety behind the windows of the building adjacent to the castle. He crouched forward along the wall and as he climbed through the window, avoiding another round of gunfire, I dashed into the castle.

Alice fired at each of us again, but she was saving her ammunition.

"Hold on!" I called and returned to the hall where I had earlier seen a closet full of rifles.

The closet was open. The long racks held Rupert's revolvers and rifles, some with special and to me incomprehensible modifications. I picked the one that seemed the most ordinary.

A sight consisting of several pieces of glass was mounted on the barrel. When I put it to my eye I realised that it was actually a telescope, permitting one to aim and shoot much farther than a conventional rifle.

Gripping the massive wooden handle of the rifle I felt a lot more secure. The bottom drawer contained boxes with bullets. I picked up a handful and quickly stuffed them in my pockets.

As I closed the glass door of the armoury I perked up. Something was wrong.

In the reflection in the glass I saw the dining room and the dead body of the headless suffragette. Except that where the unconscious Darringford should have been there was nothing. Our tussle and his defeat were marked by only a few bloody streaks.

I tightened my grip on the rifle and tiptoed into the dining room. The shield, the empty revolver, the broken dishes and overturned chairs, everything was where it should be. Except for Rupert. His bloody footsteps led to the corridor and the staircase.

I continued the search. The deadly silence did not reveal where the madman was hiding.

Monstrous ideas crept into my mind. All around me loomed high walls. Was he hiding behind a column waiting to ambush me? I cocked the rifle. The click of the lock gave off an eerie echo. Even the servants from the kitchen had disappeared upon hearing the first shots, apparently via the side entrance.

But I did not have time to waste on this degenerate lummox. Holmes was outside in a desperate situation and was waiting for my help. I prayed that Rupert had run off to his room and would leave us alone.

I backed out of the corridor and ran through the dining room to the entrance.

Cautiously I peered outside. The main gates were open, the latticework pulled back. The escape route appeared clear. But both cars were still standing in the courtyard.

Alice was sitting in her Model T and was trying to start it while keeping a watchful eye on the building where the detective was hiding. But the car would not budge. She did not notice me. She was frowning at the hood of the coughing vehicle and hitting the steering wheel.

Then I spied Holmes through one of the windows.

I motioned to him that I intended to follow her, but he waved his hand to indicate that I should not. His face was suddenly even paler. I wondered whether he had lost too much blood.

He pointed behind him and then to the countess. I understood that he was telling me that the building contained more than just buckets of feed and straw.

The detective had apparently decided to instead attempt to get back to me. But he could not do this without attracting Alice's attention. I had to cover him. I waited until he was ready and when he jumped from the window and ran across the courtyard towards me I fired in the air. Alice was startled and ducked her head. Then she took cover behind the car and fired back blindly. This was perhaps even more dangerous to us than had she taken aim. Her bullets forced Holmes to rush for cover behind the tank.

He caught his breath and motioned for me to sneak behind him. I counted Alice's shots and it seemed that she must have to reload her gun. I jumped from behind the door and with several hurried steps found myself again by the side of my friend.

"There is an entire laboratory filled with chemicals inside that building," he said. "There is enough destructive power to decimate half of Europe! We must destroy it!"

He looked at the gun in my hand and scratched his chin thoughtfully.

There was not much that we could destroy with only one rifle.

Suddenly we heard angry shouting from the window on the first floor of the castle. We turned in the direction of the sound and Alice, who also turned, cried out from her hiding place.

"Rupert, no!"

Lord Darringford stood in the window, looking like a madman. In one hand he held a stick of dynamite and in the other a lit match. He lit the fuse, laughed maniacally and threw it at us. The dynamite arched and landed near us.

It exploded and everything around us shook. A shower of clay, sand and turf fell on our heads.

"Stop you fool!" Alice yelled. "You will ruin everything!"

He heard, but did listen. He pulled out another stick of dynamite.

This one landed right near the tank. The scaffolding swayed and started to collapse. The boards rained down upon us.

Holmes coughed up dust.

"I have an idea! We must get to that tank!"

We tossed aside the boards and were soon behind the tank. We quickly found the door and opened it. Inside there was room for a two-man crew.

Rupert, infuriated that we were still alive, sought to gain a better position and view. He then noticed what I had seen earlier. The roof of the outbuilding that contained the laboratory was adjacent to the wall of the castle, making it relatively easy to attain from the window in which Darringford stood. He only needed to swing across a ledge and jump several feet below.

While he shoved sticks of dynamite into his belt and Alice yelled at him furiously from below, Holmes and I enclosed ourselves in the tank.

We gladly discovered that it was a fully functional prototype. The barrel was loaded with one shot. The controls consisted of a relatively simple system of levers.

The detective grasped them and started the tank with his good hand.

The engine roared and began to run. Alice's eyes widened and she jumped out of the car. With the tube of plans pressed closely to her breast, like a beloved child, she again started shooting at us. The bullets bounced harmlessly off the tank. From the narrow slit I saw how she turned numb.

For the first time she looked helpless.

Holmes shifted the levers and the tank slowly rumbled. The heavy truck easily dug out of the rubble of the fallen scaffolding and lurched forward.

By that time Rupert had attained the roof of the laboratory, from where he could see the whole courtyard. He lit another stick of dynamite and threw it at the tank.

At the same moment Holmes shifted the levers and drove towards Alice.

She screamed and ran to hide, but the tank ploughed into her Ford. We felt the front of the armoured vehicle lift. Through the slit the walls of the castle fell away and we saw the cloudy sky. The tracks crushed the Ford beneath them as though it were paper. Holmes then turned the tank and headed back to the laboratory.

But the madman on the roof was already lighting another stick of dynamite.

We could not wait. The detective pursed his lips and placed his hand on the cannon controls.

He aimed it at the laboratory building, on top of which the villain stood, and fired.

A gigantic projectile flew from the barrel of the tank and hit the building with incredible force. There was an enormous roar and stones cascaded in all directions. Rupert, still holding the burning explosive, yelped with surprised as the roof gave way under his feet and he fell down.

But our cannon did not kill Lord Darringford. That was accomplished by his own dynamite and the explosives which he still had in his belt.

A few seconds after he vanished into the demolished laboratory there was a large explosion followed by a series of smaller ones. We heard glass shattering, metal twisting, wood breaking and stone grating. From the ruins a fiery geyser erupted, throwing everything high into the air.

There was no way Alice's brother could have survived the blast.

An enormous black cloud of stinking gas formed above the collapsed and burning building. The hidden chemicals burned. Had they been properly mixed, even more damage would have been done. But now they simply burned and dispersed harmlessly into the air.

The courtyard was now a blackened ruin covered with splinters of wood, burning tar, grit and dust. The fire erupted, accompanied by crackling noises.

Alice was knocked to the ground by the force of the explosion.

"Rupert?" she gasped.

Fire is a good servant, but a bad master. Alice had lost her power over it.

XVII
Her Father's Daughter

I opened the hatch of the tank and looked into the courtyard where Alice Moriarty's dream was going up in smoke. A burning tuft of grass fell in my hair. I slowly pulled it out and tossed it to the ground.

I cannot describe just how tired I felt. Our sleepless night spent hurtling through the freezing darkness to Glinney, and the exhausting events following our arrival, had left me drained.

Holmes was not much better off. His crippled hand was hanging next to his body. And the most important thing still remained to be done: to retrieve the secret documents that I had turned over to Alice.

I looked around.

Alice was again on her feet. She was running towards the triplane With the tube strapped to her back.

I jumped down, but after crouching in the tight space of the tank, my old legs cramped and prevented me from moving. Thus I also blocked the way for Holmes, who cursed under his breath, giving Alice just enough time to get the propellers of the plane in motion and to clamber aboard. She did not waste any time preparing the plane for takeoff. Before we managed to scramble out of the tank the engine roared into action and the plane bounded through the gates of the castle. It picked up speed and raced onto the plain.

"Damn!" said Holmes.

"How will we catch her?" I cried. "We destroyed her car and the tank is too slow!"

Our gaze fell on Lord Darringford's car, which was covered with a tarp.

We ran over to it and tossed aside the rubble, shook off the smouldering chips that were burning holes into the tarp, and together tore it off. Untouched by the previous events the Silver Ghost now appeared before us.

"Where is the rifle with the telescopic sight?" asked the detective.

I had left it by the side of the tank when we boarded. It was now leaning against the remains of the destroyed scaffolding in the middle of the courtyard. I ran over to fetch it while Holmes started the car.

"Have you ever driven before?" I asked.

"No, but I've read about it."

"Can you manage with one hand?"

"I shall have to. I drove the tank, after all. But the rest is up to you, Watson. I cannot hold the rifle in one hand, and I could hardly pull the trigger with my crushed left index finger. I hope that you are a good shot and will not panic. England depends on you!"

It was a heavy burden.

Without further ado he motioned to me to get in, and we raced after the plane.

With the burning castle behind us we headed straight for the rolling aircraft, which was searching for a stretch of flat land from which to take off.

Holmes floored the gas pedal. Soil flew in all directions and the wheels bounced wildly as we sped highways and byways after our graceful nemesis.

We were about to reach the airplane before it got off the ground, and I was preparing the gun, when we suddenly heard a ferocious scream behind us.

I looked back and saw Alice's effeminate servant galloping after us on horseback. Apparently the smoke from the fire had caused him to return to the castle. Behind him galloped our horses, which he must have found down at the forest.

The servant beat the horse to go faster and edged ever closer to us.

"Drive faster, we have company!" I shouted to Holmes, who retorted that we were driving as fast as the car would go.

Although our car was far more powerful, the animal proved more efficient on this terrain and caught up to us.

The muscle-bound servant let go of the reins and swung his leg over the horse's back so that he could jump onto our car. I grabbed the rifle and climbed into the rear seat. I straddled the seat and waved the rifle around like a club, hoping by this mad action to drive him away.

Then our car hit a divot or a stone and I lost my balance.

I was lucky not to fall out, but I lost my footing, and one of my legs sank between the seats and got trapped. The rifle ended up on the floor.

Our adversary took advantage of the situation, swiftly loosened his feet from the stirrups and jumped into the car. While I was trying to free my leg he landed on my shoulder. But he immediately realised that Holmes was a much greater danger to him and he began clawing at him and covering his eyes. A scuffle ensued during which the blinded detective lost control of the car and it sped freely across the plain.

Alice had meanwhile finally left the ground and the plane was slowly gaining altitude.

"Watson, would you please stop playing around and get this individual off of me?" Holmes wheezed through the servant's hands.

I gathered myself and extracted my leg from the leather upholstery. Before the servant could notice, I rolled over onto my back and kicked him hard with my heel in the chin. I achieved the desired effect. He loosened his grip on the detective's head and lunged at me.

Fortunately the laws of physics were on my side. As the hulk bounded I raised my other leg, guiding them somewhere between his chest and stomach, and swung with all my strength behind me.

The inertia of his attack sent him flying over my head and out of the car.

He must have fallen hard because he lay stunned on the grass. Thus he learned just how dangerous it is to get out of a moving vehicle.

Lady Moriarty, now a safe distance away, could only watch my battle with her servant. But then she turned the plane around in a swooping ark and headed straight for us.

"She's coming back!" I cried with renewed hope.

But Holmes cursed.

The yellow triplane burst through the clouds, flying straight towards us. As it approached I could see Alice's round head in a flying helmet and goggles.

"For God's sake duck!" yelled Holmes.

Then I saw a flash on the bow of the aircraft and lumps of earth began to leap up in front of the car. I remembered the formidable armaments on the aircraft.

The machine-gun fire lasted for a few seconds before the lady flew over us. It was only a matter of time before she made the turn and swooped back for a second attack.

I grasped the rifle, aimed and fired a few times, but all the shots were off and I was forced to reload. The detective did not say anything. He knew how difficult it is to shoot an airplane from a moving car.

My hands were shaking. I probably should not admit this, but even after everything that had happened I still found it difficult to shoot the woman who at one time had meant so much to me.

Alice did not share my feelings. Again she flew over the Silver Ghost and dotted the plain around us with a hail of machine-gun fire.

But she missed us again, either due to Holmes's manoeuvres or because she did not have a lot of flying experience. But the bonnet of the car had been hit just inches from me. The hole in the canvas could just as easily have been in my stomach.

I fished two more rounds from my pocket, loaded the rifle and aimed without regret. They that sow the wind shall reap the whirlwind.

I relaxed.

It was just me, the plane and the rifle. I squinted through the telescopic sight. I could clearly see Alice Moriarty's smirking face.

I fired and hit the tail rudder. It shattered to pieces. The second shot flew wide, but the first shot was enough.

"Now she can't change direction!" Holmes cried. "She will have no choice but to land!"

The airplane swayed as Alice tried to manoeuvre in vain. Nothing helped. The machine roared above our heads and headed helplessly in the one direction that the tail wing permitted.

But she would not land. Alice had apparently decided to wager everything on her last card. She was a born fighter. Instead of descending she gained altitude. She glided over the tops of the trees in the forest beneath the plains and flew onward.

"What is she doing? How does she mean to continue without a rudder?" I said uncomprehending.

"She hopes to succeed in getting out of our reach," said the detective.

"But she will never make it! It is madness!"

"Desperate women do desperate things," he sighed. He turned the wheel and drove the car to the nearest road. "If she does not land as soon as possible, she risks catastrophe."

It was incomprehensible to me.

The plane was still visible on the horizon and was distancing itself from us. It was becoming a yellow dot against a dull sky. Holmes drove faster. We could clearly see what direction we needed to head in, but we did not want to lose sight of the plane. We could not risk that.

The road wound its way ahead through the Scottish highlands, but sometimes also got lost between steep hillsides.

The terrain did not offer Alice a place to land and so she had to continue flying.

The detective was driving so fast that the four wheels of the car were rarely on the road at the same time. At this pace the holes and puddles of the uneven road no longer presented any obstacle to our hard-charging automobile.

I had no idea what time it was. If someone told me that we had begun the ascent of the walls of Alice's fortress a few weeks ago, I would have believed it.

All of a sudden in the opposite lane I saw Tankosić driving in a horse and carriage. He was apparently heading from the train station in Glinney on his way to meet the Darringfords. Holmes saw him at the last moment and began honking wildly on the claxon.

We raced out of the turn in the opposite lane and literally swept him off the road. It was only by some miracle that he avoided us. Then his wheels slipped on the rocks and the carriage and whinnying horses fell over.

"There is nothing for you here, Tankosić!" my companion cried to him over his shoulder.

The foreigner heard his name and literally froze. But that's the last I saw of him, because we were racing ever onward. I can only assume that when his true identity had been revealed and he found the castle in ruins, he returned from whence he came. As far as I know he never met Alice Darringford.

Thanks to the frantic drive the detective had successfully managed to keep the aircraft in our sight. But as yet there was no indication that our wild chase was coming to an end. The precious documents remained out of reach.

I soon noticed that we were driving steadily downhill. The open plains of the Scottish highlands stretched ever onwards beneath us. My impression was correct. It was confirmed a moment later when we passed a sign to the valley of the Great Glen.

In front of us lay Loch Ness, famous around the world for its alleged resident, the mysterious creature known as the Loch Ness Monster.

The wind picked up and brought rain.

"She is running out of fuel," Holmes cried suddenly, not taking his eyes off the triplane.

"But she has not been in the air long," he added. "It appears you are a fine shot. You hit the fuel tank!"

The machine was nearing the jagged boundary of the horizon until it presently disappeared. But not for long. It took us a few minutes before we reached the valley, at the bottom of which lay the long narrow lake with high rocky shores. Against the background of the silvery water we saw the last moments of the flight of the yellow triplane.

With its fuel drained the machine was no longer able to stay in the air. It all turned out as Holmes had predicted.

Lady Alice's plane hit the water. Though it at first barely skimmed the surface, the force of the impact tore off the undercarriage and wheels. The airplane skipped a few times on the surface, like a flat stone tossed by a child. Then it turned a few cartwheels and the propeller fell away and sank in the water. It was a terrifying sight.

The valley echoed with the sound of the cracking hull.

The wings snapped off and ripped into pieces, lifting a wall of spray. There was an ominous splash. The geyser of water

215

enveloped the machine and its pilot before our eyes. We were too far away to help. The despair that I felt was boundless.

Waves formed on the surface of the water. For a moment air bubbles popped to the surface and then there was a long, heavy silence. We watched Alice Moriarty, like her father before her, swallowed by the cold water, never to be returned.

XVIII
The World Does Not Stop!

It began to rain and I cried with the heavens.

Holmes was mournful as well, though he did not share my grief over the death of the beautiful criminal. He was thrown into despair rather by the definitive loss of the strategic plans for the defence of England and the many important documents whose originals had burned. Many ingenious inventions thus ended at the murky bottom of Loch Ness.

It was not until the following summer that the future would in its way still find the path.

After the crash of the airplane we drove down to the banks of the lake and hired a boat. We searched the surface thoroughly, but found only bits of debris. We remained there until nightfall. In the first hours we still hoped that Alice had managed by some miracle to escape from the sinking wreckage and survive. But the water was cold, the weather unfavourable, and as time went by it was increasingly clear that our hopes were in vain. Due to her intransigence and pride, Lady Moriarty, just like the heavy fuselage of the triplane, was at the bottom of Loch Ness.

The next day Mycroft's people began to arrive. Together we searched the banks of the lake. But we did not find any traces there either. In Glinney, meanwhile, a second team arrested Alice's servant, who was grieving by the side of Rupert's remains among the rubble of the burned down castle.

We returned to London with one arrested person and reported to Mycroft. But we could only boast of a partial success: we had prevented the secret war documents from falling into enemy hands. But we had not succeeded in returning them to the King.

I must admit that Mycroft valued our achievement more than his despondent brother.

"Although we do not have the patents to the war machines, neither does Wilhelm," he said. "That is more than enough."

In any event, they had long been working on new strategic plans for the defence of the country. The risk of a breach had been far too great.

The suffragettes led by the Pankhurst clan continued to be a pressing social problem. But with the dispersion of their militant comrades we had nevertheless succeeded in declawing them. Nevertheless, they continued to promote their objectives in their own way.

As for Luigi Pascuale, his work in the factory of Vito Minutti did not last much longer after the end of our case. Mycroft sent his Italian counterpart an unofficial message full of exceedingly interesting information, which divorced Luigi not only from his lucrative position, but also for a while from his freedom.

Meanwhile Holmes and I took a several-week-long rest.

The case had been a great burden on my friend's weakened heart. I judged that if he had continued to exert himself thus just a little while longer he would have suffered another coronary. His injured hand also required care, particularly the crushed finger. With the help of experts from the clinic we succeeded in saving that too, although the detective never quite fully recovered all feeling in it.

But this was a small price to pay compared to what would have happened had I not intervened.

Unfortunately, Holmes saw it differently.

To tell the truth, since we got back to London he hardly spoke to me. He blamed my foolhardiness for the loss of the documents. For a long time he did not allow me to explain that I had only acted impulsively when I could no longer bear to witness his suffering.

We reconciled shortly before his return to Fulworth.

"*Cherchez la femme*,"[24] he said to me by way of farewell, as we embraced on the platform before he boarded the train. "Never forget it, my friend."

The phrase hung in the air as I gazed through clouds of white steam at the departing train.

---

[24] French: "Look for the woman."

Epilogue

At the end of the case I did not suspect that for the next two and a half years Holmes and I would not see each other at all or even keep up a correspondence. He did not answer my letters and I was too busy and too proud to travel to his farmstead uninvited. At first I suspected that he was simply angry at me, but the truth was actually much more prosaic. Shortly after his return to Cuckmere Haven he was visited by the minister of foreign affairs and the prime minister himself, who embroiled him in the case of a German spy named von Bork. The work occupied Holmes for more than two years and took him all the way to the United States and Canada. It all finally ended — once again with my assistance — just a few days before the Great War.

Yes, that war, which Miss Moriarty helped bring about in revenge for the death of her father and from which she sought to establish her powerful, radical offshoot of suffragettes as the rulers of an industrial empire. Our efforts, however, had not been in vain. We had delayed the conflict by a whole three years and had given England precious time to prepare. Only in our worst nightmares could we imagine the evil which threatened to destroy the world thanks to the inventions and patents for the war machines that Lady Alice wanted to build for Tankosić and other wicked men. Although Sherlock Holmes had stopped her, the new chemicals and technologies of the Great War brought death to countless thousands.

Without Holmes everything would have unfolded differently and Britain may have been reduced to ashes.

And so by way of conclusion allow me to paraphrase what the detective said at one of our last meetings just after von Bork's arrest in August 1914, when war was irreversibly at our doorstep.

"There's an east wind coming all the same, such a wind as never blew on England yet. It will be cold and bitter, and a good many of us may wither before its blast. But it's God's own wind none the less, and a cleaner, better, stronger land will lie in the sunshine when the storm has cleared."[25]

I will never forget his words.

My friend was a wise man and it was always an honour for me to be by his side. Let his words, which I have attempted to reproduce in my literary work as faithfully as possible, continue to inspire each new generation.

Dr. John H. Watson, November 11, 1927

---

[25] From "His Last Bow" (1917)

Afterword

Holmes before the Battle

That Sherlock Holmes is probably the most famous literary character of all time (at least in English letters) is thanks in large part to the measured judgment of his chronicler Dr Watson and editor Arthur Conan Doyle[26]. After all, fate and insatiable curiosity ceaselessly compelled him to leave his beloved chemistry and violin – and the quietly burning fireplace in Baker Street – to pursue cases so wide-ranging, that prudence was necessary when publishing them. Not all of them were terrifying or devastating. Many were simply too intimate or their publication incompatible with the spirit of the age or the interests of the British Empire. Doyle knew that Watson could not yet publish them, despite the fact that he had recorded them. That they really happened is testified only by cursory mentions in several published cases.

The "good giant", as the French nicknamed Doyle, generously gave his successors the opportunity to write what he had not yet had the chance to publish. In addition to the gaps in time between the various stories, which are being gradually filled in thanks to the unrelenting zeal of his "pupils", the works contain exciting references to an entirely unknown world of other Holmes cases, which Watson, despite the clamour, in his devoted zeal simply had to record. An unexpected legacy of

---

[26] Father Ronald A. Knox invented a popular game called Holmesology, which is based on the belief that Sherlock Holmes and Dr. Watson were real people and that their stories form a canon of literature from which it is possible to reconstruct their lives.

Watson's manuscripts is therefore constantly being discovered in suitcases and boxes found in attics or bank safes. The wind of time has spread many of his stories throughout the world. The sheer number of stories makes one wonder when he found time for his medical practice. Let us leave the answer to the researchers, the men and women who love Sherlock Holmes.

Their approaches are of course very diverse. This is best seen in the anthologies of stories, such as the now nearly classic *Murder, My Dear Watson: New Tales of Sherlock Holmes*, *Murder in Baker Street* and *The Ghosts in Baker Street* by the trio of John Lellenberg, Daniel Stashower and Martin H. Greenberg. Indeed, in the foreword to the first of these we learn why the approach of some of the authors towards the Great Detective borders on the disrespectful and sometimes even the sacrilegious. I do not mean all of the parodies which appeared in Doyle's lifetime (and which amused him greatly), but those stories in which Holmes is expropriated by the author for other purposes. Their *raison d'être* derives from Doyle's capacity for measured judgment.

But he also knew how to make provisions, and so around 1899 he entrusted Holmes into the care of the most famous American actor and playwright of the day, William Gillette. With Doyle's blessing Gillette used parts of various Sherlock Holmes stories to piece together an excellent melodrama, which became a Broadway hit and then a nationwide sensation. The play enjoyed similar success in England and after performances in London toured the British Isles and Europe. At one point while writing the script Gillette sent Doyle a telegram asking whether it would be all right if Holmes married. The author's reply would give future writers of Holmes stories practically unlimited freedom: "You can marry him, kill him, whatever you wish." Thus Gillette ended his play with a certain Alice Faulkner in Holmes's arms. If today we do as we wish with the character of Sherlock Holmes, it is, with all due respect, Arthur Conan Doyle himself who is to blame.[27]

Although the original Holmes cases were often precisely set in a certain era or were at least classifiable[28], they nevertheless existed in a kind of timelessness without social weight, in the pleasant comfort of a politically indifferent jolly old England, despite Doyle's well-known civic activism. Holmes's only directly political engagement in *His Last Bow* (published in *The Strand Magazine* in September 1917) was a mere, albeit sincere, patriotic demonstration by its author. Doyle for good reasons wished his readers to believe in an ideal justice, a non-partisan Sherlock Holmes. As we said, he knew had to exercise measured judgment, and did not want to risk compromising his publishers or endangering his civic activities and reputation. Therefore his later stories often take place in the past, in the nostalgic atmosphere of an extended Victorian era. From today's point of view, he wished himself, his readers and England peace in which to do their work.

From this point of view the most provocative Holmes adventures are not the new ones that deal with the figure of the Great Detective (such as David Stuart Davies in *Double Game on Baker Street* or Petr Macek in *The Golem's Shadow*), but those that locate Holmes in the present day. Donald Thomas thus in his *The Secret Cases of Sherlock Holmes* and in *Sherlock*

<hr>

[27] See *Murder, My Dear Watson: New Tales of Sherlock Holmes*.
[28] See *Sherlock Holmes of Baker Street: A life of the world's first consulting detective* by William S. Baring-Gould.

Holmes and the Running Noose had Holmes solve real criminal cases of that time. Imagine how exciting a portrayal of the sad trial of Oscar Wilde would be under the pen of Dr Watson! Perhaps one day such a text will be discovered. Or a confrontation between Sherlock Holmes and Jack the Ripper, described more satisfactorily than by William S. Baring-Gould in *Sherlock Holmes of Baker Street: A life of the world's first consulting detective.*

Of course, these are cases involving just historical individuals. In the book which you have just finished reading, Mackenzie Peterson has had the audacity to pit Holmes against a political movement. This is, at least to my knowledge, a fundamental breakthrough. Holmes, despite his reputed aloofness with regards to women (with the exception of Irene Adler) and to society generally, here comes up against the limits of his iron-like determination. He was not much impressed by Marx following a chance encounter with him in the British Museum Library in 1877, even though he acquainted the detective with the London group of Russian anarchists[29], but now Holmes could not avoid discussion of the accuracy or even the legitimacy of his actions in investigating the strange case.

Where did the trail, leading initially to the Reichenbach Falls, actually go? He marched to it with a purpose, towards a battle for life and death, knowing, however, that it would be a battle against one man. Now he stands against the interests of a socially deprived group, whose demands, he must admit, are just. Better our modern recognition that the suffragettes employed means on the borders of the law not only out of

---

[29] At least according to William S. Baring-Gould in *Sherlock Holmes of Baker Street: A life of the world's first consulting detective.*

fanaticism, though they are sometimes comic and sometimes dangerous, but also from true desperation over the rigidity of society, and even more tragically, their position, as in their misery they were manipulated by the personal psychoses of one woman hell bent on revenge. Fortunately, however, this revenge was not properly chilled. The mind of Holmes's charming counterpart flickered with the mad flame of entrepreneurial megalomania, and when she was swallowed by the waters of Loch Ness, the Great Detective could be congratulated for extinguishing, at least for a time, a much more frightening flame – the flame of war.

Boris Mysliveček, editor, the Czech edition of the book

Also from MX Publishing

MX Publishing is the world's largest specialist Sherlock Holmes publisher, with over a hundred titles and fifty authors creating the latest in Sherlock Holmes fiction and non-fiction.

From traditional short stories and novels to travel guides and quiz books, MX Publishing cater for all Holmes fans.

The collection includes leading titles such as *Benedict Cumberbatch In Transition* and *The Norwood Author* which won the 2011 Howlett Award (Sherlock Holmes Book of the Year).

MX Publishing also has one of the largest communities of Holmes fans on Facebook with regular contributions from dozens of authors.

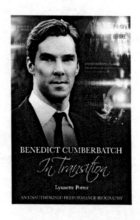

www.mxpublishing.com

Also from MX Publishing

Sherlock Holmes Short Story Collections

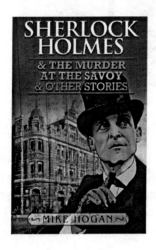 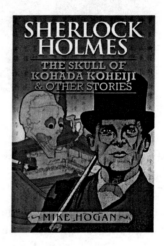

Sherlock Holmes and the Murder at the Savoy

Sherlock Holmes and the Skull of Kohada Koheiji

Look out for the new novel from Mike Hogan
– *The Scottish Question.*

www.mxpublishing.com

Also from MX Publishing

Our bestselling books are our short story collections;

'Lost Stories of Sherlock Holmes' , 'The Outstanding Mysteries of Sherlock Holmes', The Papers of Sherlock Holmes Volume 1 and 2, 'Untold Adventures of Sherlock Holmes' (and the sequel 'Studies in Legacy) and 'Sherlock Holmes in Pursuit', 'The Cotswold Werewolf and Other Stories of Sherlock Holmes' – and many more......

www.mxpublishing.com

Links

MX Publishing are proud to support the Save Undershaw campaign – the campaign to save and restore Sir Arthur Conan Doyle's former home. Undershaw is where he brought Sherlock Holmes back to life, and should be preserved for future generations of Holmes fans.

Save Undershaw	www.saveundershaw.com
Sherlockology	www.sherlockology.com
MX Publishing	www.mxpublishing.com

You can read more about Sir Arthur Conan Doyle and Undershaw in Alistair Duncan's book (share of royalties to the Undershaw Preservation Trust) – *An Entirely New Country* and in the amazing compilation Sherlock's Home – The Empty House (all royalties to the Trust).

Lightning Source UK Ltd.
Milton Keynes UK
UKOW04f0312130914

238480UK00001B/15/P